THE

BLUESIANA SNAKE  FESTIVAL

THE
BLUESIANA
SNAKE
FESTIVAL

· A NOVEL ·

Aubrey Bart

COUNTERPOINT

BERKELEY

Library of Congress Cataloging-in-Publication Data

Bart, Aubrey.
The Bluesiana snake festival : a novel / by Aubrey Bart.
p. cm.
ISBN-13: 978-1-58243-577-0
ISBN-10: 1-58243-577-4
1. New Orleans (La.)—Fiction.
2. Music—Louisiana—New Orleans—Fiction. I. Title.

PS3602.A8384B57 2010
813'.6—dc22

2009052551

Cover design by Kimberly Glyder Design
Interior Design by Elyse Strongin, Neuwirth & Associates, Inc.

Printed in the United States of America

COUNTERPOINT
BERKELEY
2117 Fourth Street
Suite D
Berkeley, CA 94710

www.counterpointpress.com

Distributed by Publishers Group West

10 9 8 7 6 5 4 3 2 1

. . . Probably many a road scholar would testify this place makes good leavin and better comin back to . . . Place puts a hold on your soul, man, these streets call you like an old song . . . Yeah . . . Way downriver, heart of a swamp, she's a city made of music, down soft ground between memory and dream . . . Ain' no gettin down like the gettin down got down here, you gotta get it . . . Downriverway down womb of the land down subsealevel gets down as down gets, man—moon over this place puts heads thru changes . . . World comes in feedback rarefied down subsealevel, you get into this kinduva dream-am-I-dreamin-or-dream-dreamin-me sorta shuffle . . . Awta be official state headspace is what it awta . . . Deepspace propers down sameway pelicans get to be state bird, man, some quantum hype we're onto here . . . Lord knows people up and down these streets make living proof does being here contact buzz immaculate . . . Only makes sense people holdin offthewall karma would funk off here . . . Yeah, we've seen the saga . . . Pilgrim don't know you're a pilgrim, y'know, you're passin thru town . . . So you're passin thru and you're passin thru and you keep on passin thru, y'know . . . Days come round, you've gotten all but gone—somebody's pilgrim done gone new wave native . . . Happens here like it happens noplace else . . . Regular function at the junction all these people having moments people have only here . . . Popular creed comes off any excuse for a party or parade . . . That's howcome you see all this roleplaying, all these masquerade scenes around here . . . People get into it . . . Unlived lives break loose on these streets, man, whatcha don't see here ain't happenin . . . Shadows outta closets put stories on the streets that's a preholy city true to form—man, you wear that out you ain't never lied . . . . . . Weird . . . . . . Coulda swore I caught that thought on the fly, now I'm flashin on some other time I dreamed it . . .

—Hidden Dave Crossway
Jungian streetsweep

THE
BLUESIANA
SNAKE
FESTIVAL

I

The Quarter

We weren't spaced out, we were in this
spaced out place, and we knew it . . .

—Brooklyn Bob Ravenscroft

Midsummer snakemoon blue on bluesiana

Down joint down old Decatur Street, place called The Boss Fix Jam. Passway backfume the Elysian Fields bus offbound winding low. Shrouded coffin overhung the bar shot spoof aura shadowfall a ceilingfan. Weddingparty aftermath somebody's bridegroom spunout facedown in the weddingcake. Jukebox rhapsody *"loving you has made me bananas."*

Vernon "Dickinthedirt" Rappaport pulpiteering: "Whodat bungholed by a loose canon called american dream?"

Thanks for the inspiration, brother Dickinthedirt

Big Jim Bullshit slingin that hootch—he's about to pick up the phone: "Who ain't here? Finney, you here?"

The Beadlady, in whitewig over mock polyester black, leans indoors with her new cajun a-rab impression: "Anybody owe me money?"

Big Jim Bullshit, hustlebustin face on, pointing street, ran her—"Fuck she think dis is? comin in here widdat jive coonass."

"She's talkin in tongues, BJimBu." Voice of Matt Dockery drinking off discovery his untenured job was listed in the want ads (stone Joycefreak—claimed he could tell from the passage what the master had been drinking, sometimes even switches of pleasure thru rewrites). Couple live ones he had buttonholed, husband and wife out of Montreal. He's waxing native son, talking his town—heels of The Beadlady, some man in peestained floodlength candystripe pants, bellying to the bar, puts a touch on:

"Would you believe it?"

"Probably not."

"Sixty-nine cent more buys me a bottle of Mulekick."

"Mulekick!"

"You betcha."

"Sweet Jesus have mercy—blood spiked with that shit probably rids lice."

"Done worse dry, brother."

Big Jim Bullshit put the hook to the hustle. Dockery profiled slipping the man fivespot while the two live ones scrambled cameras ready.

Passing hoofbeats foregoing carriagewheels

(Her take) "The French Quarter is probably as old world as the old world itself anymore."

(His take on her take) "Not to mention otherworldly as the next world at that."

(Dockery's pearl) "To a city true to its ghosts—"

Do me like you do, Big Jim

You want dat greasecutter, dawlin?

Gimme all ya got, honey

You got dat muthafucka! (slamdown hipside bottle to rockglass)
I love it!

Compliments of the house for streetcrew. Minutes come midnight over coffee for the soul: Milo Kopke down on a jewsharp bought off some old man at the flea market; Beverly Griffin a paperback found in the street; George Forbert, to his wont, a pipe.

Bellylaugh out Bev, look cut Milo: "I see what you mean about the understated humor in this."

Milo said, "Paperback trance in progress," and turned twangs in a ditty.

Story over Milo's head on this one:

. . . lift in a squad car, next exit ramp: skinhead haircut, ten days inside (busted for weirdness passed off a turnpike hitchhiking rap) . . . impounded backpack light a couple items (paperback trance to soften the rub of that nickelbag ditched highwayside) . . . proof of God no Selective Service trace . . .

Jukebox bangin Beethoven's Fifth; backtable jewsharp accompaniment.

Chartbuster with a bullet!

Forbert grinning pipesmoke.

In sashays Shushubaby to the strains of "My Man" feeling-shape *I heard that* subscape *Alvin Lee in her room with his shoes off* Strutting city issue orangeflare over formfaithful jeans; workgloves one hand, cigarette and walkingcup the other: "These two dudes I just met turned me on to some amolnitrate."

Milo said, "A friendship to be cultivated!"

"Really. They were coming outta The Lantern hanging all over each other, y'know. I said, Can I walk with you? I was afraid I might freak'em out, y'know, being too bold or whatever, but they were sweet as could be. 'Sure, honey, you come with us. Anybody gives us any trouble, three screams're better than two!'"

Herecome Hidden Dave Crossway—Jungian streetsweep working to support a writing habit (his novel *Lovers and Other Dirty Fighters* soon to be published soon as he got a publisher). Blowed from far look: shades, scarf, whichway hair. Comes off with the shades to hang out with Shushubaby (she was his friend who got him on the street crew): "Years now I've been hearing about this *El Topo* flick. Gotta see *El Topo*, man. Raise your consciousness untold megaherz. Elbow slippin the armrest woke me up. I walked out . . ."

Tommy Blaha didn't just make a scene, he stormed it. Shirtless. Jeans cut off to a tease. Androgyne tattoo active with keenings of his streamlined, boldly notched physique. (Somebody once said Blaha was born on an offramp . . . *son of a wild man and a wilder woman.*) Comes in full swagger ahead Liz Klutch and Albert Johnson—him fuming, them laughing.

"He got kicked out of The Toulouse for yelling at James Booker to cut the jive and play!" Matronly in bibs, backbun and grannies, Liz Klutch had somebody's oldfashioned auntie covered—

They kicked'im out for that?

"Oh yes, dear. James Booker gets kidgloves treatment in there, you better believe it."

"Hi Albert!" Shushubaby's kinda man, Albert Johnson: black dude tall and slim, erect on his bones, loose at the joints. He set her fresh coffee, she like to blushed: "Oh, how sweet!"

Albert that Albert smile eyebright like a woman: "How sweet it is! I spilled the sugar."

Already Blaha had seen enough, "Later for this," he was walking, lay siege on the pinball machine over Got Grease Grill across the street.

". . . Well, let me tell you, James Booker fa-reaked. He's on like the apron of the stage, okay. 'I'm rappin up the people, man.' Tommy goes, 'I don't wanna hear it.' Really. I'm like, I am not be*lie*ving this. They're having *words* over people's *heads*. It was *rude*."

Doc showed up with Brooklyn Bob; Doc a dark moon on, head hung, hands in pockets; Brooklyn Bob taking measure all around, attitude *It seldom matters* Doc aka Alan Updock, lapsed biker out of Detroit, at forty the elder statesman of the streetcrew; Brooklyn Bob no streetsweeper but more like streetcrew emeritus by reason he was a chessplayer.

"Doc just got a ground zero street rap laid on'im."

Doc broke it down: "I'm walkin down Ursalines, comin down here, I see these two bros crossin the street up ahead. So one of'em I see bends down and picks somethin up off the street. He's showin his partner, y'know, they're into this thing. So I'm makin the corner, dude asks me do I have a light, and he's, you know, sorta lettin me see this joint that he's found. I figured I'd help'em out, I give the dude a light, then he offers me a hit. I'm like, Hey, y'know, this is all right. I'm thankin'em, y'know, I'm about to take a hit, I look and the other dude has a pistol on me. They got these cocky smirks now, right, dude tells me, 'Go head, take a hit,' he says, 'You wanna be feelin good as you can for this.'"

Now was Brooklyn Bob got a smirk: "Mightcoulda passed it back when they hitch'up for yer money, Doc. Be feelin good as they could for zero large!"

Albert come lately: "I write a mean IOU!"

Big Jim Bullshit would know what was more: "You heard about Dirty Ernie got mugged up on Bienville. Didn't have no money so they took his hat."

United Cab Ronnie stopped in for a break. "Just got stiffed on a fare upto The Funk Shop. Some kid AWOL from the military, man. I mean talk about a storyteller. 'DI was an asshole, man. I went over the wall.' Weapon goes off at inspection, right. DI was on his case. Anyway, upto The Funk Shop I'm pickin up he's slow from the pocket, right. I get this sinking feeling about the fare. Sure enough he cops a plea. I'm flashin on Future Winos of America decab here, right? I mean what could I say? Yeah, hey, no problem, kid. Thanks for the tax writeoff. Then he's hittin on me do I have anything for the head! I'm like, Hey, I don't mix business with pleasure, okay? Specially when business is slow. He goes, Hey, that's the best time. I said, Out. Then he makes with this touch like he's down on hard times, y'know, would I lay some paper on'im! I said, The most expensive fare I've had in I dunno how long and you have the gall to panhandle? He goes, You gonna be cool or what?

I mean d'you believe 'at shit? I said, Work up a juggling act, kid. He bends back on my finger and goes out slammin the door."

Marlies Hennegar, waitress upto Mespero's, brooding off Immigration hassles:

"Never have I felt such freedom as I feel here . . . I so do not want to leave, but I may have no choice."

Guy bellies barside; glazed look, random air, eyecontact call this was not his first stop. Said please for a draught, reaching for his wallet. Big Jim Bullshit took the style hit. One draught up in a frosted stein.

Longwayfromhome look about Marlies would not escape notice.

"I was once a man who moved patrols thru jungles."

Burnout to one comes in a place and gets weird with somebody mightcould apply. Lifestories she could tolerate, provided you kept it positive; patrols thru jungles could be told someone else. When he stayed with the subject, she shined him on. He rambled on anyway. Something about three slugs caught in a firestorm . . . carried out the jungle on a buddy's shoulders. Talking at her face in a barback mirror got him stonewalled same in remove. His voice shook; shook and broke. Crosslooks offmirror cut fluterank forefronted. Guy was in tears but not finished yet. Something about the few who got out alive. She turned facing him—the mug slipped his grip, dumping on photogear up bartop. Big Jim Bullshit slipped Dockery topsops. The stranger made apologies, but these people had no time for imbalanced behavior: apologies met same as patrols thru jungles. Big Jim Bullshit told the man come see him tomorrow; he stood him a fresh draw—this time in a plastic walkingcup. The stranger slumped, face in hand. Marlies just looked at the guy. Dockery and the live ones too. Was Milo Kopke brought the coverage. United Cab Ronnie was with him; Brooklyn Bob and Forbert too.

Milo long and spindly at his flamingo pose on one leg: "Care to join with us in headship?"

The stranger wiped his mug a backhand: "Good stuff, dude?"

Hidden Dave Crossway got up to go, got waylayed by this cameracarrying couple coming tableside. The woman was ample who once had been fine, winter blonde, smile more timely than felt: "Excuse me, you people sweep the streets, I understand?"

Dockery was all over the coverage: "They wanna get some pictures, I told'em I'd get'em some local play."

Crossway led with his eyes: "Pictures don't turn out, you still been anywhere?"

Mugs hung *wha?*

Crossway had it behind him, he was walking. Doorway out he crossed passing nods with Poopdeck Perry of Baltimore.

Big Jim Bullshit spotted Poopdeck Perry: "*Ah-right P Doop!*"

Poopdeck Perry faced off High Noon style: "You cajun muva!"

"Whodat bungholed—"

Wear it out, Dickinthedirt

Dockery got next Liz Klutch: "So whatta we got for a moonswoon vigil? Go go or no go?"

Liz shrugged: "Beats me, dear. The square is open but the lights are still on. Hard to tell who, what or even if at this point."

"Max wax is when?"

"Threethirtythree, dear."

"Max wax at threethirtythree. Kind of a numerological ring to that."

"Really."

GreatGoneBefore

Liz Klutch and Albert Johnson kicked back at Place d'Armes:

"Whatever happened to the proverbial bath of moonlight?"

"Sounds like one for the grafitti wall, dear."

"Personally I find the cathedral overenhanced. In my view all of this artificial light is a desecration. I could feature undeflected moonlight anytime."

"Weird thing about it probably most tourists could too."

"The powers that be should be persuaded of the sheer vanity of all this kilowattage."

"Albert, you're such a romantic."

"Diehard innocence groping in futility."

"I love it!"

Dockery said, "You know, I heard someone say, This is snakemoon, you know. I'm thinkin, No, I don't know. What is snakemoon? I dunno, d'you?"

Liz said, "Search me, dear. Sounds swamp culture to me, but then again it could be an indian thing or something, I really don't know."

"I detect pop astrology."

"Truth to tell, dear, for all I know, somebody just made it up."

Meantime, at a wayside salvaged Baptist pew, United Cab Ronnie was schooling Dockery's live ones: "Yeah, style counts for a lot in this town."

The weddingparty holdover, somebody's bridegroom, stirring from stupor, bid a rally; weddingcake wipeoff wanting wiped more, he was heard muttering slurred: "Wants she should get on my case I'm a loser? Well I got news for her: If ever there was a asshole there was hope for, it's gotta be me, and I'll swear by that to my dying day, and I don't mean what's left of it."

Crosslooks and highsigns *so much for any good to come of a Boss Fix nuptial bash*

Couple-three flicks at a lightswitch. Big Jim Bullshit hailed the house: "Daddy's feelin happy but he's runnin outta tricks!"

Everybody heard that.

Place was bedlam.

Keep it lit, pass it around

—Graffitti wall, Ursalines Convent

Fountain plaza benchtop ("Torrid florid" surround): Milo sparked a bone and passed it.

Brooklyn Bob said to Art Nieman, "Y'know I once asked a California dude howcome California people are so weird. He said, 'It's the fault, man. All that earth energy comin up from the fault.'"

Art Nieman said, "There's an old California saying: At the end of the trail, you're bound to see some horseshit."

Brooklyn Bob had to laugh: "I like that!"

. . . Chopped hog winds out on Decatur

Nieman said, "So whattayou guys do here anyway?"

Brooklyn Bob said, "I don't, they do."

Milo said, "Actually we're in trash."

Nieman said, "A straight job?"

Milo nodded: "Streetsweep."

Nieman: "Awyeah? That's cool. Y'know I've heard tell streetsweeps in San Francisco bring down fifteen large a year."

Milo said, "Not this side of truth."

Nieman said, "Hey, what you bring down brings you down, hey, I don't need to bring it up, know what I'm sayin?"

Milo said, "Put it to ya this way. Anybody workin for the man for less is doin time inside or on a chain 'n' anklebrace outside."

Nieman said, "Hey, that's cool. You're into an alternative lifestyle."

Brooklyn Bob said, "I foresee a Tomb of the Zen Wageslave

all the rage at The Oddfellows Cemetery."

. . . The Beadlady slinks crossplaza

United Cab Ronnie asked Nieman, "So howya like this mother of midways?"

Nieman said, "Mother of midways is right. So far I've dropped fivespot to some black kid bet he could tell where I got my shoes. Then I got about threefourths tight on somebody's bootleg absinthe. Then just now I caught the bum's rush outta this place over here."

Forbert said, "I fell for that shoe gimmick once. It was a long time ago. I didn't pay up though."

Nieman said, "The walkingcup was what bummed me out."

Brooklyn Bob said, "Big Jim Bullshit sayin it with plastic. Now there's one for the ages ever I heard one."

Nieman said, "I had all my shit packed. Nobody wanted to hear it."

Brooklyn Bob said, "Hey. Hot timin town, man. Yer gonna get eightysixed. It happens, y'know. You take it in stride."

Nieman said, "Big Jim Bullshit, uh?"

Brooklyn Bob said, "Operates black 'n' white, recollects in technicolor."

Nieman said, "No harm in that—I hope."

United Cab Ronnie said, "Claims he got shook down by Elvis at an airport."

Nieman said, "An airport?"

United Cab Ronnie said, "Claims Elvis flashed that G-Man tin, y'know, that Nixon laid on'im?"

Nieman said, "Shook down by honorary heat all shook up."

United Cab Ronnie said, "Vintage BJimBu."

. . . offriver whiff of mud airs trace heartland

Nieman said, "So where you guys from?"

Brooklyn Bob said, "Better from than there."

Nieman nodded: "Hearya there. Been to the mountaintop, seen the compromised land."

Brooklyn Bob said, "There it is."

United Cab Ronnie said, "Not the land of a thousand dances."

Brooklyn Bob said, "More like night of the living dead turns to day."

United Cab Ronnie said, "Your basic mainstream american slobocratic lifestyle in other words."

Nieman said, "So this is asylum."

Brooklyn Bob said, "Ass end of the river, man."

United Cab Ronnie said, "Bottom landing right here."

Milo said, "You follow a voice till you come to the music."

Nieman said, "Hearya there, man. I can definitely relate to that."

Milo said, "What we're onto here is this plane at a frequency unlike anyplace else above ground."

Nieman said, "Man, I dunno where your realityspace is at, but it can't be crowded."

Brooklyn Bob said, "Yeah, ole Milo, he's pretty stretched out."

Nieman said, "Principled dude."

Brooklyn Bob said, "He's like an old tree. I mean if anybody can exist without a witness, Milo he's got balance in the dark."

Milo said, "Speakin of the dark, I'm flashin on lights out for the people at the square."

United Cab Ronnie said, "Kinduva guerrilla moonlight

observance in the making, more or less."

Nieman said, "Radical."

United Cab Ronnie said, "Uncut moonlight is the buzz."

Nieman said, "Do I detect counter tourism?"

United Cab Ronnie said, "Imagine Deja Vu instead of hors d'oeuvres."

Nieman said, "Which way to where this is at?"

Milo said, "You can come naked."

Nieman said to Milo, "Y'know, I could swear I've seen you before."

Milo said, "Ever done—course you haven't done time, what am I talkin about?"

Nieman said, "Never done time, but I have done active duty."

Brooklyn Bob said, "Hey, we're all inmates or out, know what I'm sayin?"

Nieman asked Milo, "Ever in country any chance?"

Milo shook it off: "Declined my invitation."

Nieman nodded, "Hearya there. Served 'n' damn proud of it, don' gimme wrong, but I don't hold nothin gainst nobody for shinin that one on."

Milo said, "You did your duty, I did mine."

Brooklyn Bob said, "Talk about inmates or out, I did active duty *and* time."

Nieman said, "You served in the military?"

Brooklyn Bob said, "Private first class. Got my Parris Island pin. My Korean War Service Medal. Can't fake them trimmings, man. Did I serve in the military."

Forbert said to Nieman, "I didn't believe it either at first."

Brooklyn Bob said, "My honorable discharge should be

as believable as his Section 8 Deferment."

Nieman said, "I believe ya, man."

Brooklyn Bob said, "All of eighteen when I enlisted. Fresh outta high school. Awyeah, I was gung ho, boy. Strictly John F. Wayne."

Nieman said, "John fuckin Wayne! Ahright, you are a grunt!"

Comprehensive brother handshake . . .

> *Hey, if you don't believe The Babe really called*
> *his shot, you damnside best had believe he meant to.*
> —Calvin "Bobo" Proffit

Concrete breakwater, foreyard Esplanade Wharf, down old Peter Street, opposite the French Market arcade;

. . . Wayside wallfront, shadowactive: parked cars outlined in crosstown headlights . . . metamakes, riderless, trace on the spook (to refer suchlike nextlight):

Scratchbuilt toolshed offlit from the produce arcade across the street; *CLOSED* handpainted letterimperfect on the door; assets in store: pushbrooms and binshovels long on wear, workgloves indeterminately stashed or discarded. (Toolshed under padlock, pushcarts on a chain, shape of issue what it was, inviting spoof; but like the bossman Bobo Proffit would say, "Not everybody comes to church to pray.")

Pickup white with amber dome, Sanitation emblem either door: Bobo Proffit at the wheel—traveled bush hat, day or so stubble—vanishing sixpack at hand, singing *Don' fuh-get ah Mon-day date* . . .

"Bananas" Joe Bonomo brooding foursquare at Proffit's window: thumbs hitched in pockets, attitude *Ain't dis some shit*

Day ago morningshift some old woman hosing shopfront pavement turned the hose on two of Joe's crew and when Joe went to see whatdafuck and the old woman turned the hose on him Joe went upside her head. Now Joe was a fallen labor advocate and Proffit's time had come: Proffit would be replacing Joe head of French

Quarter street sweeping operations and Joe replacing Proffit head of this detail shitbottom of the municipal power structure (Joe claimed he stepped down).

The transfer of power met mixed reactions in the ranks:

The man's a pathological fuckup, man

Yeah, well, we're an equal opportunity outfit

He suckerpunched an old lady, man, I mean how insecure izzat?

Joe overcompensates

Proffit called it shape up, like they call it on the docks—workaday connection hung on this crew to be cute. ("Hippiz with jobs ain't hippiz or ain't jobs—look again.")

Liz Klutch would find Proffit hale if not well met: "Carrotcake, Bobo. Homemade."

"You know ah don't eat nuttin hippiz make."

"Oh for heavensake."

"No tellin what konna locoweed you people put'n somp'n like 'at."

"Far be it from me to shake your serenity, dear."

Proffit stepped out the truck, stood full height—back-bend loosen some truckseat out him—not to see fifty again though still a fair figure of the onetime sandlot mainstay used to make backhand stops, drive balls over heads ("Nothin beats a bat 'n'ya hands, a cigar outcha mouth 'n'a cold one in the cooler . . ."): Inch or so upward six foot, sturdy underbite, brew yet to tell round the middle (once got tossed for dusting the due batter during warmups).

Shushubaby stepped forward: "Bobo, can I have new gloves? These're grody."

"No baby, y'can't. Ah jiss gaveya dem."

"I know you did. I need new ones already. These leave prints."

"Woish'em if dey doity."

"I did. They're still disgusting."

Blaha said, "Give the girl the gloves, Bobo."

Shushubaby said, "I'm ashamed to have these in public."

Albert had gloved up, tweaked fingertiphold one of Shushubaby's gloves: "We're talking germ signatures from some of the most intense gutters in the city."

Proffit said, "Woish y'hans bafaw y'go handlin y'sevs y'won't be gittin no goims aboutcha. 'At's what crotchrot's all about. Hippiz don't knowdat."

Blaha said, "Yer talkin outtayer ass, Bobo."

"Awta be glad a whatcha got, y'ass me. Wudn' no new gloves eva mont when ah woiked ott hehh. We brought ah own uh we did widout, simple azzat."

Albert said, "Reflections of a golden age!"

Blaha: "Give the girl the gloves, Bobo."

Proffit cut Blaha a look not trained on redeeming qualities: "Tommy, if ah gitchu a seaman's cawd, wouldjou take a ship?"

"Pack it dirty, Bobo."

Albert said, "Strictly short time shippers, thank you," and Liz got a husky laugh. Albert said, "Select bars afford boarding privileges in kind."

Proffit said, "Yeah, ah'll betchu da pride o' d'fleet, awncha?"

Albert said, "Keep your contacts for someone who can't make it on a ship without a seaman's card."

Liz yukked, "I love it!"

Not one to linger in a downhill conversation, Proffit got

a line on a whole other drift, eavesdropping only so long, then homing in for the strafe: "'At's like da one about da fella pulls a gun 'n' sez, 'Awrightchu muttastickas, dis is a fuckup.' I'm tellinya, somebody wanna git hisself laughed off a cellblock pullin a stunt like 'at. Holdin up a streetsweepa fa Godsake, whoeva hoida such a thing? I'll tellya one goddamn thing, you think you caught da hindmost—ma good friend Thibidoux got mugged by some bulldyke disguised like one a dem Krishnas. Yeah. You huyd about da bulldyke disguised like a Krishna. You ain't huyd about da bulldyke disguised like a Krishna? Mugged ma friend Thibidoux right up hehh on Rampawt Street. Put a shitkickin on'im, too, umma teyya what. Thibidoux he couldn't unnestan it. He thought it wuz one a dem Krishnas, see. Come to fon ott it was a bulldyke in disguise."

Albert said, "Sub-Saharan ancestry, no doubt," and people laughed.

Mimic rattletrap all along the wallfront: ashtruck hitting on about half its cylinders; dumpbody percussion every pothole. Engine idle upto halfminute after shutoff.

Driver out the Ninth Ward, Leo Dazzolini: sagging figure in bargain threads fitting somewhat; hands downside, toothless pidgin tongue, tried eyes out worldview by lowbeam. Shed the trademark porkpie lid he mightcould slip recognition.

"No Rudolph 'n' Clyde?"

"Ah waited twenny minith, Bobo. Ath wha ahm late."

"Why'n y'pick up y'radio? Ah been callin ah dunno how long."

"Radio buthit, Bobo."

"Ya radio's busted!"

"Ah tolya bout dat."

"You neva tole me nuttin bot no radio."

"Ah tolyadat, Bobo."

"Y'tolme da hahdrolik wudn' right 'n' ah had dat looked at."

"At wuth night bafaw ah tolya bot d'hahdrolik, Bobo. Memba lath night ah come inna Humminboid . . . you'n Brotha Boike . . ."

"Yeah, yeah—"

"Ath when ah tolya bot d'radio wudn' woikin."

"Ahright ahready. Putcha name onna timesheet, Dazzlin."

"Wudn' f'dem otha two ah'd a been heh on time, Bobo."

"Think ah didn' have at figgid up front? At's how come y'don't see dem pushcawts dumped way dey at, ah got news fuyya."

Beverly Griffin stepped up: "I'll volunteer for the truck."

Leo beamed: "You'll woik wit me, Beb?"

Proffit jammed Bev: "Pushin a broom in the street ain' man enough fuyya?"

Bev said, "If I were a man it wouldn't matter, would it, Proffit?"

Proffit shrugged: "Don't make me no diffence. Be too confusin if it did."

Liz screened Bev; back her off, cool her out.

The pushcarts wanted dumped before operations got underway.

Somebody said, "Who's gettin up in the truck?"

Proffit said, "C'mon, somebody git up'eh, be nice."

Doc made it topside.

Detachable cans, two per cart, for the hefting:

Tighten up, Doc.

Crossway and Blaha hefted one, then another; heavy metal rung on the slamhome. Bev stood ready to gear in with Albert. First can went up without a hitch, but the next only so high and almost back down but for Doc at his reach to weigh the save.

Proffit yelled, "C'mah, git doze cans up eh. Y'gawna break d'man's back makin'im gotudda well like 'at."

Bev dropped back, next can all Albert, she was taking off her gloves. She drew full height, hand behind, twist and bow, see could she work out her back, short favoring it. Proffit was watching. She cocked him a snoot—hand at her back passed off strictly casual, strictly unconscious attitude. Crossway, on looksee, brought Albert coverage, no hitch in the getalong. Was Bev broke eye contact—jump steady at the toolshed.

Proffit said, "No maw volunteeh f'da truck?" He had this smirk now. "Wha hapna volunteen f'da truck?"

Bev said, "Change of heart, Proffit?"

Proffit said, "Less jess say ahm impressed wit what ah seen."

A pushcart jamming ragged blacktop took Blaha flush on the shin; he pitched a fit: one after the other over the tailgate with the cans, then over the wall with the pushcart.

Proffit said, "Wanna git dat cawt back heh while you still got a job, son?"

"Bullshit Bobo. You want proper work, get us some proper equipment out here."

"Back heah widdat cawt or yo fired."

Blaha read Proffit to filth every step of the way. Last word went down with the pushcart retrieved under protest: "Ahm puttin you on notice, son. One maw fuckup 'n' you betta be streetwise, unnestan?"

Johnny Albesharpe swung the market arch in his maroon '67 Galaxy 500; with his usual showtime stop next Proffit's truck, the trademark driverside exit feature was in effect (door wouldn't open/window wouldn't close). Johnny would be the latest of a streetcrew succession of lapsed scholars (termpaper short a bachelor's in anthropology). What was more, his senior ranking on upward four years tenure was far an alltime streetcrew consecutive service record (compared, say, to Blaha's five years in three tours).

Proffit said, "Saddy night late again."

Albesharpe shrugged, "Oldies radio, Bobo. No way I can break away before midnight, what can I tellya?"

"Well ah'll tell you somp'n, son. From now on, you ain' hyeh fa quatuh afta, you will git mawked absent 'n' you won't git paid, unnestan?"

"Can't do that, Bobo."

"Awyeah? Well you jess see what ah can uh can't do when ya paycheck comes in light."

Albesharpe shook it off, "I got sick days, I got personal days."

"Dat's immaturial." (A Bobospeak buzzword: immaterial.)

"Tell Civil Service that."

"Ah'll tell Civil Soivice same as ahm tellin you, son, don' make me no fuckin diffence."

Hidden Dave Crossway took mock indignant: "I do no be-*lieve* that I am hearing this particular language at a municipal depot."

Albert Johnson said, "I share my colleague's outrage at such indescriminate use of double negatives."

Albesharpe smirked, "King's English with a yattitude!"

Proffit said, "Yeah you right, ah don't dot ma oz—but

ah do git read—so roll 'at 'n'ya zigzags 'n' nevamind."

Leo came forward, forefinger for begpardon: "Ahm takin Beb, Bobo, no kiddin?"

Proffit smirked, "Y'wanna putcha gloves on you gonna take Bev."

Liz snapped, "Ca-*rude*, Bobo," and Shushubaby said, "Really."

Leo flustered, "Ath not what ah meant, you know betta'n 'at. Hith makin 'at up. You awful, y'knowdat? Ain' he awful?"

"Ahright ahready. Evabody present 'n' unaccounted fuh? (Bobospeak read hippies did everything stoned.) Ahright, hezza deal. You pickin up Boibon Street—"

Say fuckin what?

"Da sweepa machine is down."

Saturday night again!

Hidden Dave Crossway spoke up: "Sir, in the words of the Big Bopper, and I quote: 'But . . . but . . . but . . .'"

Proffit told Crossway, "You woik wit Milo." He cut Milo a smirk. "Ya pawdna voluntidda woik onna truck, wudn'at nice?"

Crossway told Milo, "Not the breakthrough it appears. Do not be unduly impressed."

Proffit said, "Awyeah 'n' Fognoggin (Forbert), by d'way, ah got anotha complaint from the hotel. See datcha all git dat got, y'hear?"

Doc heard that. "Dammit, Proffit, we're not hotel help. Hotel garbage is hotel work. Where do they get off puttin it on us?"

"Some folks is f'doin, some folks is done fuh, whattaya gonna do?"

"Dogs 'n' garbagemen scatter hotel garbage, we're

supposed to sweep it up?"

"Routine heroics, Doc."

Doc went away mad.

"Heah you people talk you'd think y'had real jobs uh somp'n. Ah neva seen maw people wanna blow an easy setup cuz it ain't easy enough. Awta be backin up to pick up y'paychecks as it is."

. . . *Tour carriage rolling by, driver at his rap:* "Know wha d'French Mawket neva close?"

Blaha, Liz and Johnny amped off: "Because it has no doors!"

Carriagedriver rolled with it: "Yeah you right. It have no doze . . ."

Blaha hollered in their wake: "You ain' never lied!"

Womanvoice in the carriage: "Who are those people?"

. . . *brainchild of some local shaker and mover name of Ken Pope, advocate for Quarterpeople earning wages keeping the Quarter kept, the duly formed Vieux Carre Task Force came to be known as Proffit's hippies . . .*

Proffit said, "Ahright ahready, go git it got." (Vintage Bobospeak, "Get it got"—by some lights the "Hippocratic Oath of streetsweepery.")

Hidden Dave moved out at a fetchdown sixties slouch, dragging his broom, whistling off his *Marche Slave/Enigma Variations* medley . . .

. . . *Appointed rounds east of midnight, pavements heart of town, pushbrooms and cartwheels made nightmusic for the soul . . .*

II

East of Midnight

It's all about hearing the music
—Grafitti Wall, Ursalines Convent

All nights are weird in the Quarter . . .
The moon is like the file in the gumbo.

—Beverly Griffin

Could be, as some believe, this was not just any old Mississippi
Moon on any old Southern Night.

Was Doc once described Leo Dazzolini "the fastfood of
lifestory." Told untold tellings at that. This time to memory
by dashboard light:

". . . Utha be ah could do heaby woik, Beb. Nod no maw.
Ahm twenny yeath dithablt 'coun' ah almoth died. Ah
tolya bot dat feeba ah caught dat time?"

"I think you did."

"Crawd und' a howt wit no thoit on? Flea offn a rat bit
me, gimma d'feeba real bad? Ah tolyadat ahready?"

"You told me."

"Dawt ah had it dat time, Beb. Dawt ath a gawna. Know
wha ma tempitha wa? Hunnud'n fob. Belieb 'at? Gawth
hawneth trufe, Beb. Hunnud'n fob ma tempitha wa. Deh
didn' know wuth ah gonna make it. Hadda kimma on ite
kimma from boinin up. Thing ahm kiddin? Feeba like ta

boin me t'a crip, betta belieb it. Magine 'at, Beb? Little
bitty flea offn a rat done all 'at. Eight yeath ath outta woik.
Atha long time, Beb. Eight yeath otta woik a long time.
Ain' no good cummadat, umma teyya. Ahd rutha woik,
me. Ahm thebm night a week ott hehh, y'know."

"I know. You should take a night off."

"Who me? You kiddin me, Beb? What umma doof a
night off? Ah dunno ta do of mathef."

"Take it easy."

"You kiddin me again, Beb? Nah. I don' mine woikin.
Gimma ott d'howt. Gimma thumna do. Twenny-fob yeath
ah got wid Thanatathin, y'know. Gone on twenny-thik.
Awta be thutty-tree, only ah almoth died like 'at. Took alot
outta me, Beb, betta belieb it. Ah ain' beena thame thinth."

"Nobody's the same as they used to be, Leo."

"Ath a powful man when ath young, Beb, you kin ath
anybody. Ah got all ith fat now, but ath a powful man when
ath young, betta belieb it. Utha be ah could take a
phonebook—you know how big a phonebook ith.
Phonebook like 'at! Utha be ah could take a phonebook 'n'
rip it in two. Ath putty powful, Beb. Ain't dat powful?"

"It's powerful all right."

"Ith a trick to it, Beb, ahm not gonna la t'ya. Ith a trick
to rip a phonebook in two. Know howta do it? Know howta
rip a phonebook in two? A page at a time!"

Gutbucketbust out Leo fetched Bev a grin.

Leo was downshifting, swing up St. Louis Street, Trans
Am coming otherway cut him off at the fork—

"Aw yeah?" He punched it. "Thummabith."

"Leo, take it easy."

He like to powershifted—wound it out wide open. Trans

Am was all taillights: upto Chartres Street, gone across it; pursuit barely halfblock.

"Thummabith!"

"Leo, calm down."

The streetsweeping mission covered crosstreets and backstreets then Bourbon Street to the gutterbottoms for collection by dumptruck or sweeper machine. A getdown crew could get it got, and these people were and did.

. . . Down Chartres Street Forbert and Doc got sidetracked watching some funkoff get down on a poledance with a balcony support . . .

Something dead in the cart been dead a long time—proof them that push carts keep downwind the gutter by proxy.

Doc had his own style pushing a cart: bentover low, carthandle one hand, shovel to pavement otherhand—sweep and scoop in one. He's down some Decatur Street gutterbottom with this act, some outlier blowed off the american highway on a chopped hog got off this rap some longlegged blonde he had picked up (and dropped off) middle of the Mojave Desert told him next moon down this town would be righteous. Forbert and Doc pointed him straight to Jackson Square . . . (*landmark specter of hogs end to end the tour carriage stand fencerowfront old Decatur Street.*)

Threshold the old Hibernia building Forbert left off some bottle deposit action for winos to scoop (Willie Woe and the boys would know where to look). Man in the peestained floodlength candystripe pants (put the fivespot touch on Dockery over The Boss Fix) turns up curbside:

"I just got the shit beat outta me. Bastards took my last five bucks."

Forbert and Doc just looked at each other.

Milo had this thing about his inner sound on Bourbon Street. Figured anybody could hear the inner sound in this sensory swarm had to be turning high frequency. He's sweeping curbside, listening could he hear—bearded man in monkcassock says to him, "God gives us simple tasks, and when we do those well, He gives us harder ones." Meantime Milo up with the broomhead, put right a misbrush on a soulbrother's walkingshoe—dude spit on broombristles (ward off arrest). Milo said sorry, and the bro, flash grin/snap soulfist, cutaway cool; nextbreath Milo turned the Man of God prayered hands, said, "Service without striving."

Royal Street at St. Peter a Great Dane on hindlegs upside a Volkswagon bus barking at Tommy Blaha up on the roof.

Doorman over Pat O'Brien's calls crosstreet: "Brotha, you dogfood he gets holda you!"

". . . holda my broomstick I'd skewer the—"

Barking gets heated.

Fairskin baldheaded man, goldhoops leftlobe, leans out A&P: "Tippy, honey, pleaze, lower profile—"

"Get this dog off my case, man."

Look on the man's face prefiguring later telling over cocktails *My God, he's treed Tarzan!*

Local light outside Johnny White's calls downstreet: "Hey man, listen to me, if he's been neutered, go ahead 'n' make a break for it, hear?"

Doorman over Pat O's: "Go back t'da Nint' Ward, Joe Don Bourre."

"Hey, I'm serious, man. My ex-ole lady useta train dogs, I know what I'm talkin bout."

Tommy said, "Man, if this dog don't have balls, I don't even wanna know if he ever did!"

Barking, barking, barking all the *while . . .*

"Tippy, honey, now pleaze. I'm asking for cooperation. *Ask hell, I'm insisting!*"

What Hidden Dave Crossway could do with a pushbroom was a texan in a tengallon hat could tell: "Podna, you shootin a mean stick!"

Still with the shades to the pale of the moon; necksash turned headrag worn barbary style for the street—

Suit attack out Port of Call; eyecontact call *budding captains of industry and their girlfriday dates*; latitude *uptown comes French Quarter slumming*

"Business pickin up?"

Shine on   *straight lift from the public domain passed off like his own mindmade pearl*

"How much they pay you for this?"

Attitude   *Ain't nobody's business but my own*

"The man's talkin to you, streetsweep."

"Better to sweep trash than talk it."

Younglady steps down in the gutter, "C'mon," but her date slips the handhold.

Crossway off with the shades—

Other fella smirking: "You're cool."

Younglady upcurbside told Crossway: "I feel sorry for you."

Crossway led with his eyes: "Stay in one place forever."

Fella said, "Same to you, pal."

Ladies front and back held off the young turk. Hidden Dave made back on with the shades; put to rights a garbagepile parted by parting kick. Milo, handy with the pushcart, hung *wha?* Hidden Dave shortened on the stick; he was walking.

Driveby glimpse up a balcony of castilian wrought iron: man with a bucketful of bills on a string tormenting a man down gutterbottom holding onto his hat

". . . Ah don' lub ma wife. Theth a good woman, don' gimma wrong. Ath fawty-faw when ah got marrid. Ath lonely. We neba had no chillen uh nuttin. Feeba fik me tho ah can' ha' no chillen. Didn' take ma naytha, dho. Ah till got ma naytha. Beb, can ah thpreth mathef?"

"Leo, you don't have to watch what you say with me."

"Ah don' mean no dithrethpek uh nuttin."

"I know that. Say what you feel. Whatever you wanna say."

"Prethiate it, Beb. Ah prethiate dat. You gonna dink ahm awful, but ahm not gonna la t'ya. Ah don' ha' nutna doof ma wife. Ma wife nine yeath olda'n me. Theth thikthy-two, gone on thikthy-tree. Atha ole woman, Beb. Thitha ole woman when ah marrid uh. Theth had it. You laugh!"

"I know. I shouldn't."

Dumpsite, Dauphine Street, Leo swung curbside; up with the dumpbody, down tailgate clearance. Citytime he was offtruck putting word on the street: "Proffith out tonight." No sooner said, Proffit busted the scene: stage a stakeout. Bev and Johnny hefting cans held his watchful eye.

"What's Bobo's trip?"

"The heavy lifting act."

"Your basic psychomanagement style in progress."

"As in bent on me faltering and him being there to get off on it."

"You know where that's comin from."

. . . *honey out of Illinois called Toona. Route all her own, no designated partner (itself an irregularity wanting watched) . . . Dateline Leo dumpsite to next, situation alert: Toona's pushcart outside her apartment, Proffit's pickup parked round the corner, eyecontact call any fool. Was Bev backed Proffit to the wall on this. Shape up next night she let him know people weren't digging what was happening. Hear Liz Klutch tell it: He fa-reaked! Proffit's wife (somebody's Ma Hatfield lookalike) showed up—would hardly be anything left to call good after she got thru with this. Toona walked, not about to look back (Hidden Dave Crossway would be her replacement). Later in the night, at Nellie's, up Rampart Street, Proffit, in his cups, took Johnny in his confidence: "Ah love ma wife, but she don't gimme no head, see. Toona, baw, she'll gitcha rowin witcha feet . . ."*

> You would have to be pushing a broom to find
> Bourbon Street sobering.
>
> —Albert Johnson

Bodyheat overshrouds midway Bourbon Street, image swampscud lamplit under. Neon midnighthouring musk vapors. People passing people in the night. Bouquet of deepfry. Of spiked passionfruit. Now and then a wharfwaft trace abroad: coffee, molasses, essence of waterfront. Promise of wide open hot times in the air. Music out doorways, music on the street, music offriver, music out of nowhere. Here an Elvis impersonator, here a Louis Armstrong imitator, this corner Frogman Henry shades of Fats Domino. One man eightpiece band in a harness pulls off a resemblance to "The Marseilles" on request. Down by the riverside "Dixie" on calliope; ragtime steamboat whistleblasts key of G. Singsong monotone adrift in the throngs: "Buy my poetry—it's good enough to wrap your garbage in." Threepackaday sandpapervoice barker doorfront Big Daddy's cuts some Alfred E. Neuman lookalike peekpurchase buxom proof of life after Storyville. Full throated Biblethumper calling it down: "Praise the Lord and hold onto your pants." Hustlers dressed all manner of undress strut their stuff and profile. Barefoot man in black feeds folks gibberish meaningful to somebody not met yet. The Beadlady peddles luckybeads: two bucks for mojo, one for souvenirs. Hotrod angel shirt to shoes foul of puke pitches refund at a hotdog vendor having none of it. Womanchild with a duck in tow gives it all new meaning or else no matter. Down this town streets are lined with fastfood wrappers and throwaway walkingcups. Streetsweeps bring back sidewalks and gutterbottoms for the people.

• • •

Albert Johnson was broomslinging downgutterbottom, chair thru windowfront over Dugan's Beanwagon put a sideshow on the street—exit some waiter not looking back. Herecome Tommy Blaha keen for the skinny. "An escalated career choice" was the spin Albert put on it. Blaha retrieved the furniture, and Albert swept the fallout.

Somebody stuck a rose on the pushcart Liz was pushing.

"Whazzis I hear about a citizen's initiative at Jackson Square?"

"Well, nobody knows what's happening, dear, but everybody I talk to is gonna be there."

Ruthie the Ducklady in leotards and tutu, shooting the throngs on rollerskates, boombox upside her head, freehand describing a prelude. Some systems analyst on the loose from the hinterland, spoofing in her face, amuse his companions: Ruthie busted his mug a coldcocking fetched from waydownhome—like to spun out on the skates but didn't dump (center of gravity cradling the boombox). Blaha brought coverage but the showoff stood shown. The companions howled. "Pinhead by TKO!"

Ruthie had it behind her already, skatewheels rolling, boombox blasting, handjive philharmonic.

Street evangelist testifying corner of Bourbon and Orleans: "Could I blow like Joshua, I'd jump the secondline! I'd cakewalk souls to glory blowin ragtime! God of Abraham, here's what I say. Ragtime for deadfolk. Out with muffled drums . . ."

Aside God of Abraham would only be Hidden Dave
Crossway paying attention. He recognized the preacherman from some time ago down Beale Street in Memphis
preaching Elvis freed more people than Moses. On reflection
the preacherman would swear he could recollect Hidden
Dave or a lookalike in shades same as now only no headrag
or broom. Hidden Dave told the preacherman thanks for
the inspiration, and the preacherman told Hidden Dave
God bless the streetcrew.

Max Tron's mobile tictactoe unit was all the rage on the
street. Challenge to the sporting public: match wits with
the Grand Master—bantam rooster name of Deacon John.
Fiddler Ron could be heard dispensing commentary: "It's
a house wheel, man, know what I'm sayin? I gotta hand it
to Max . . ."

Johnny Albesharpe stood all he could; he made his move,
show this Deacon cock *Not in this house*

Fiddler Ron saw it coming. "Uh-oh, look at this. I don't
believe it! He's layiniz money down. Aw man, I can't stand
it . . ."

Johnny played to the crowd, played it cool; played
percentage tictactoe, strictly calculated man against cock
passed off effortless lark.

The Deacon took Johnny out citytime, no contest. Upto
threeplay limit Johnny laid his money down—got lit up
every time.

Fiddler Ron fell out: "Somebody come get me—I'm
helpless."

• • •

Dumpsite down old Decatur Street; no trace of Forbert or Doc: Leo and Bev turned cans over tailgate then Leo put the cans to rights and Bev stowed the pushbroom and shovel.

"The hellayou been? you sonuvabitch." Betty Booty, friend of Leo's out the Ninth Ward: bottle redhead, puffy round the eyes; midriff spread once grinding trim.

"Betty—"

"Donchu Betty me, buster. Ahm two nights runnin a tab over here cuzzayou, goddammit."

"Ah fuggot all abot it, Betty, honeth ah did."

"Ma ass you fuggot."

"You know me betta'n 'at."

"All ah know is ma goddamn beer is warm 'n'it ain't been paid fa."

"Be right ova, heah?"

"In a pig's eye, buster."

"You hoid what ah tolyadat otha time, dinya?"

"Yeah 'n' you rememba where ah kickedja, doncha? you wanna be smawt."

"You a bitta woman, Betty."

Bev got walking. Leo called her name. Horselaugh out Betty echoed balconybottoms.

"Be right back, Leo. Go ahead settle with your talent."

"Don't knock it, honey. It don't last a minute 'n'it pays the rent."

"Y'need t'quiet down, Betty, ahm tellinya now."

"Packs by the ounce, pays by the pound!"

"Y'pithin me off, Betty."

Bev cut over The Funk Shop round the corner up St. Philip Street. Forbert and Doc were at a table in the courtyard. It was

John Stern, figmentist painter, eating popcorn; Rolf Eisemann, continental socialist, sipping burgundy; and Matt Dockery still down on his native son jam with the two live ones.

Forbert asked Bev, "How's it goin with Leo?"

Bev nodded, "He's holding up his end of the conversation."

Doc said, "Heard the bit about the fever yet?"

"Quite a bit, actually."

"Hundred 'n' four on ice."

"Hundred 'n' five."

Forbert said, "So much for coolin out Leo."

Dockery said, "Hey, we all know how that one goes. Like my ex-wife useta say: The older you get, the hotter you were."

Proffit came got Forbert and Doc for movement on the hotel complaint mentioned at shape up. Getting that got about filled the pushcart. Doc was livid. Soon as Proffit was gone they made it back over The Funk Shop. Fiddler Ron and Henry Delzell were on hand with war stories from the street music scene.

Delzell staged an impromptu gypsy fiddle serenade.

Fiddler Ron and Forbert sat down to a chess match. Forbert moved straight for his endgame but his A game went out of him and left the fiddler back from the dead. Somebody said a Gainesville gambit Fiddler Ron pulled out his ass.

Assembled gallery, all of two, WWOZ jock Al Finkelstein and Master Grill and Deepfry Chef Timetrappin Tom Hill, hung on an upset in the making.

Midpassage Delzell left off the fiddle.

Grin Fiddler Ron got goofed on heavy weather ahead: "Uh, George."

Proffit alert took bets off the board. He cut the highsign, Forbert and Doc stepped outside. Fiddler Ron and Timetrappin Tom tagged along. Proffit talked breakdown of curbside safekeeping: "You'd hafta be educated to do somp'n stupid azzis." Evidence their pushcart drovedown broke off telltale patchburns of somebody's brokenfield parkingspace maneuvers.

Forbert said, "The garbage looks familiar."

Sudden development, otherside the street: Man in peestained floodlength candystripe pants, knocked out on a doorstoop (done down on Mulekick—reflex whiplash headbutt tripped a door alarm). Man just nodded no matter the alarm. Time for trouble even in his sleep.

Parish tank guest of the DA in the forecast—this accidental prowler was about to draw coverage like he would never know. Beverage enticement, compliments of The Funk Shop (brokered by Timetrappin Tom), scored Proffit's kind offices. They stowed the subject backbed the pickup and split under cover of municipal service. Time came the alarm quit but the cops never did post. (Now what to do with the outrider?)

On account of the pushcart got scrapped, Proffit directed a shakeup. Bev went back on her regular route with Milo, and Forbert and Doc joined Leo on the truck. Hidden Dave switched off to Albesharpe and Shushubaby.

At Molly's up Toulouse Street Hidden Dave took Bev on the Q.T.: "So a backache wasn't as entertaining as somebody expected!"

Bev said, "I didn't think anybody knew."

"He knew."

"How did you know?"

"I knew he knew when he said he was impressed."

"You saw it all."

"I saw some good work on that truck tonight."

Was a comrades in brooms embrace got joined.

Out on Bourbon Street some brother hit up Shushubaby for a smoke and a spark—one pitch led to another:

"Say baby, look hyah. Whawayou say if ah wuz to eat yo pusseh?"

"No thanks."

"Coun ahm black."

"Man, I've had black dudes."

"Ah*right*. Baby down widdat blood action, baby say. Say baby, listen ahm sayin. Ahm comin straight to ya, baby, hyeh wuttum sayin?"

"Your dick isn't big enough."

"Whatchu say?"

"You heard me."

"Go head, girl."

"Later, dude."

"C'mon roun hyeh umma show ya way issat."

"Forget it, man."

"You ain' gotta be no fret."

"Maaan . . ."

Catchhold, come along, sidestreetside, palm the package.

"I've seen enough."

"Go head, girl."

"Give yourself a handjob, man."

"Damn, girl."

Bev and Milo down on Bourbon Street, curbside Takee Outee. Pistolshot inside. Man drops counterside. Outbounder into his pants with his piece say, "This is a capgun." Made off downstreet cornerround and gone.

Milo said, "Did you hear what he said to me?"

Bev said, "I thought he was talking to me."

"Where were you?"

"Right behind you."

The penny you aint got
May as well be horseshit
In a two car garage

—*"Day Old Blues"*
Furman "Bootlip" Russell

. . . *You might say the blues make gospel in heat sameway sex makes holy promise. At pulse code of feelgood feeling in the body, naturalfact is the blues pulse the code.*

Something of the blues lay foreshadowed in The Book of Psalms when Babylonian captors ask their slaves for songs of mirth from Zion. Latterday folks feel raw blues catch Holy Spirit in gutbucket strains of soul memory. That what's in boogie chillen what's gotta come out. It's what the delta minstrels were all about . . . In our time like no other time the oppressed people liberate the oppressors. That's the blues and nothin but the blues. Straight. No chaser. Amen.

—Figaro cover story
by The Royal Street Sage

Bootlip's guitar may sound simple, and it is; but for untold knockoff attempts thru the years, that Bootlip sound might as well be a phantom locomotive whistle.

—Sage in the *FIG*

Down joint down St. Peter Street, place called Moondip Minnie's. Took its name from a figure of Storyville renown. Blues headliner Bootlip Russell put The Dip in a happening way. The streetcrew turned out full strength—including Proffit (outrider still backbed his pickup) and Joe Bananas (warming up to stepping down) and even Leo Dazzolini (was doing better but got over it).

Opening act was Daytime Johnny Omen. White boy off the Jersey Turnpike downriver to play the blues. Decked in his trademark fedora with a nighthawk feather, he turned loose licks on a Mississippi National Steel, paying Bootlip goodfaith propers a hardworking *"Kick Lawanda Kick."*

Hidden Dave Crossway put it sidelong by United Cab Ronnie: "Pre-Parchman." (Reference to Bootlip's formative songwriting upto the pivotal chaingang experience according to the *Figaro* cover story.)

Table offside the bar Bootlip Russell took it light, saying hey at wellwishers; sidekick some round man in tailored threads name of Sook Coleman, got a wideangle tweak on a fat cigar. Blonde in black name of Pamela Conn and Vernon Dickinthedirt Rappaport rounded out the inner circle. Pamela was down from Memphis staying with her sister Louise (Broussard) on Barracks Street in the Quarter; was Pamela and her other sister (Shushubaby) went down the station, took Bootlip down off the train. Dickinthedirt, late of Memphis, was longtime drinkingbuddies with Pamela's squeeze. These folks and Bootlip went back years gone nevermind (had to be Who's Who pull got Dickinthedirt past the door here on account he was eightysixed at The Dip).

Sook Coleman let liploose his cigar come Shushubaby and some looktobe streetsweeps in orangeflare same as her.

Shushubaby say to Sook, "We thought since Bootlip useta sweep streets, too, y'know, maybe he might like one of our t-shirts. You know, like honorary streetcrew or whatever."

Gutbucketyuk out Sook. "Eh Boodlyup . . . Eh Boodlyup."

Bootlip fix his mark to his mug to cover of somebody's *Figaro*; turnsee what it is, say hey at Shushubaby.

"Eh, look hyah, deeze eh folks sweeps da streets."

"Awyeah?"

"Yeah, er-uh, you a honoraruh sweep! *Heh!Hyah!Hyeh!*"

"Well bless ma soul!"

Shushubaby passed Bootlip standard issue one size fits all, Sanitation emblem and letters black on orangeflare.

"Well glory be!"

Shushubaby ask could they buy him a drink; Bootlip heard that. The Dip served Prohibition style, in jamjars, and Mia slinging hootch poured wetter than not.

Buzz at the door greeted Sweet Emma Barrow here from her engagement upto Preservation Hall. Folks wheeled her offside say hey at Bootlip. They talked a spell. Bootlip ask Sweet Emma would she sit in.

Meantime Daytime Johnny was all showtime. Could be ticket off Jackson Square and choice corners wayside Royal Street. Aside a "Derivative Johnny" aside people give the boy love. Wound up told thank you and all but unplugged.

Sweet Emma got brought by a standup piano. Sound off some keys, she got a face on. Dust trap sound like to her ain't never knowd tune.

Bootlip heard that say, "Lord have mercy."

Sweet Emma heard that heard: "You ain' never lie."

Hidden Dave Crossway did a Casey Kasem: "Who woulda thunk it? A Bootlip–Sweet Emma superjam in the making! Stand by for a Dixieland–Delta Blues fusion experience you won't wanna miss!"

A man and his guitar under a bare lightbulb took The Dip deep tonk.

Bootlip took his torment to the people: "Dat boy make me look so bad."

Nahhhhh . . . No way

Daytime Johnny holler: "You're the man!"

Bootlip reached for the jamjar, call it sugarwater; slug him some like a true believer. Sweet Emma took a dim view such no account. Bootlip cock her a look, caught a look cock him same. Bootlip mug for the people, toss off stagewhispers.

Sweet Emma tell him, "Don't no jivetalk cook no beans 'n' rice, honey."

Bootlip heard that. Look like to him gal talkin him turkey set to make off with his room. Time he throw down them hardproof blues.

Opening bars of *"Snakebite and Rosey"* Hidden Dave and United Cab Ronnie crossed knowing looks: *Post-Parchman to burn!*

Was Bootlip's chops all over the place, somebody said better Sweet Emma had a drumkit. Some wit enthused, "Lay down those crossover figures!" Bootlip got back his recollection middle of singing off *"Blind Eye Winkin"* tune of *"Snakebite and Rosey."* Damnside mixup raise hell with timing. Best leave loose this number, fetch up that jamjar.

Quit on, left lone, Sweet Emma took salty: "Da hell konna mess wuzzat?"

"Yeah, ah wuz, er-uh, playin tune wit de pe-anner whut ah wuz."

"At's *hat* sorry!"

Jamjar offerup: "Oil what ails, honey."

"Aw hush up dat! *(Bootlip cueing yuks)* Pity 'n'a shame!"

Bootlip bid another number, redeem hisself, but the bluenotes done gone jamjars dried. No chance hearing

Sweet Emma keep hurtin time, she was holding all ivory, waitsee would he give or would he go. Bootlip go down choppin—

Pamela Conn holler: "Get'im! Get'im!"

Was Dickinthedirt Rappaport just did spare an ass over guitarneck rollover. Milo Kopke helped set the man straight.

Don't be Sweet Emma holdin out much hope say: "He done. He done."

Bootlip must had Papa Legba at his back. Bated guitar from downhome hold the house. Tune of *"A Ambush Callit Life"* turn other words:

Aw Sweet Emma, Aw Sweet Emma you mean
Aw Sweet Emma, Aw Sweet Emma you mean
Evabody say so, Aw Sweet Emma you

"Get'im! Get'im!"

Folks helped the man off to a rousing sendoff, he worked up a wave going away: "Did ah do ahright?"

Sweet Emma look away, shake her head, heard to say: "He ain' figgid wuz he upto count a nine or woke up to a dead issue."

Woman called Bebe, head help upto Buster Holmes', way out the door, say, "Them blues wuz booze 'n' nothin but the booze."

Hidden Dave nodded, "Wuzza one we bought'im brought'im down, but it wuzzis hellhouse audience made a minstrel scene out of it."

Daytime Johnny had put away his guitar, got hold Bootlip's instead. This was one hardtraveled, long gone outta tune blues axe. Down the groove, Sweet Emma pounded some barrelhouse eightyeight, Daytime Johnny fingerpicked straightlift *"No Account Blues"* and Sweet Emma sang this once only song don't nobody call by name:

> *They say his calls gives womens the crawls,*
> *his calls gives womens the crawls*
> *Whodat calls give no womens no crawls?*
> *Honk his snores honk onliest calls he call*
> *Must be them womens they frogs*
>
> *Temme it ain't so, temme it ain't so*
> *Temme it ain't so uh jess go*
>
> *Temme it ain't so, temme it ain't so*
> *Aw don' temma nuttin, temma nuttin*
> *Jess go*

(Someways back of beyond callit Zion, Moondip Minnie know that old ragtime ain't never lied.)

St. Peter upside Dauphine

Albesharpe sweeping runningside, Hidden Dave parkingside; Shushubaby on the pushcart with the scoop act . . .

Nontraditional Mississippi queen calls crosstreet at three bros and two white girls: "Hey, anybody needs a partner there, I'm partypeople."

Brovoice comeback: "Suck what?"

Salt 'n' pepper scene moves indoors.

Volunteer sashays doorfront, chins off a peepsee thru a fanlight transom—beersplash in the face blurs lamps every time . . .

Place called Myrti's, St. Louis upto Burgundy: battened creole in spanish stucco, cornerfront french doors; red light outside, lowlight inside. Drag scene. Soul.

Ramone on tour, make the block, shake some trade. Baby got the rhythm in her feet, got it goin on baby do—K&B Chantelle wig, Function hiphuggers, Pas de Deux fuckme pumps—baby down. Latemodel compact cruisin longside *whiteass windashoppa mekkin me peekaboo been on ma shit from Conti Street* Ramone profile, crook knee, akimbo: "Don't even botha if you don't have a big dick, you muthafucka you." Dude move some carlengths, stop, be waitin. Ramone walk on by; dude move, be longside. She stop, he do. "Muth* fuck* you, muthafuck!" No sudden move: pop purse, pull ordnance, put away some peekaboo— couple slugs in his tires. Cruisecar sag in the street— somebody's whiteass hellbent upstreet (better said there he goes than there he lies).

Drag queens out Myrti's looksee what it is—

Herecome Ramone say, "Dude peekaboo me gonna see somp'n, baby, ah pawked his ass."

Creole queen couple-three inch upward sixfoot called Natalie say, "Girl, you be bringin some heat down on us, pullin 'at piece arown hyeh, wussa matta witchu?"

"Dude don' make me no play wanna go they own way, baby, ah'll send'em, me."

"Send shit, girl. You ain' send nuffin. Fuckin caw blockin traffic gonna mess up some trade—"

"Da *fuck* wrong witchu, girl? Worrin me bout no heat 'n' no trade, you git *out* ma face wit dat shit, *nah.*"

"Da *fuck* you talkin me worrin you bout nuffin, girl, don' *be* no trade lok it gawna be heat, wha konna shit izzat?"

"Girl, ah got plans."

"Sheet."

"Yo ass."

"Yo momma want it."

"Yo momma workin Camp Street, *bitch.*"

"Aw *suck* a dick, bitch, ah feel fuyyou."

"Girl, donchu *tell* me to suck no damn dick when you ain' had no oppa-ration, *bitch.*"

Herecome Hidden Dave and Johnny Albesharpe: "Everything cool here?"

We cool, baby. You cool?

Come Shushubaby in a sweat: "We heard shots."

Ramone singsong Shushubaby: "Awww, they ma girl! Gimme some sugah, baby. Ahrightah*riiiiight*! So ha y'all doin? Y'all wurkin hawd?"

(Pistol shitbottom this pushcart could defy shakedown)

• • •

No compliments of no house for no streetcrew no kinda way; Myrti's one joint streetcrew lay they money down. Shushubaby feed the jukebox; shake it down with Natalie and Desiree. Albesharpe grease down on porkchop and turnipgreens. Hidden Dave stand Ramone doubleshot her pleasure (Ramone on the phone talkin doubleparked vehicle to Central).

. . . Silhouettes boogie off a shevoice softsoft on a bassline

Ramone sip her drink thru a straw, party that bar end to other. Ramone hang with Hidden Dave, they get a spoof on:

"S'a bad muthafuckin play dude wanna mess wit me af' ah fown out ma fuckin ass is pregnant."

"That man leave you in trouble again?"

"Go head, dude."

"Ain' no konna way."

"Ahm tellinya."

"Wanna keepya barefoot 'n' pregnant what he wanna."

"You know it too?"

"That man ain' doin you right."

"You ain' neva lie. Thang Gyawd ahm not Cathlik—ah kin git 'n'abawtion it won't be no sin."

Shushubaby groove tableside, hit up Albesharpe a bite off his plate.

Ramone say, "Hey, y'all, look hyeh, ah wanna bah y'all a drank, whattayall drankin?"

Shushubaby make the bathroom; Ramone make the bar. Natalie tableside, keep that beat shook; Albesharpe cut her a nod, look away, scope some dancefloor, scope out window way. Natalie scope Albesharpe scope hisself away; grin cut him face on and face only, meantime keep time.

Ramone bring back a round, hang out awhile her and Natalie.

"Say baby, look hyah. You know somebody trade some homegrown uh Mexican mebbe fuh two lids Hawaiian?"

Albesharpe need that one run by again. Natalie and Ramone gotta laugh.

Herecome Shushubaby back with happening bathroom for the telling: "That was weird. I mean it was *weird*. They were layin this trip on me in there, y'know. *'Fish. Do it standin, fish.'* Weirded me out, man."

"Aw fuck dem bitches, baby. Don' pay'em no mind."

Albesharpe retrozoned: "Hawaiian for Mexican is herb for weed, man. That don't make."

Shushubaby hung *wha?* "Did I miss somethin?"

"Go head, baby. Say, temma somp'n good, baby say. Yeah you right. Look hyeh, y'all. We ennatainuz, dig? We be mixin wit people, das ah thang. You know me, ahm alwiz feelin fine. Somp'n keep a good head on, we doin it, dig? Check it out, y'all. Dis shit we got *too* heavy, dig? Ah mean it *heavy*. Ah smoke dat shit ah be gittin all wozz 'n' shit. Be *real*ozzin thangs. 'At don' mekkit on 'iz cawna, baby. Dis a action cawna dis hyeh, dig wuttum sayin? You comin ott hyeh wit a pawty buzz on . . ."

Myrti her ownself, slingin that hootch, slipslide offside Shushubaby:

"Whazzis ah hyeh bout snakemoon down Jackson Square?"

"Beats me. Something about turning off the lights or somethin, that's all I know. All this snakemoon stuff, whatever that is, that's all new to me, I've never heard of that before."

"Snakemoon sound like hoodoo to me."

"Hey, tell it to somebody who knows hoodoo like you do—I don't."

"Honey, you listen ahm sayin, when themthey drums beat that snakemoon, you wanna be someplace outside hearin."

"You trying to weird me out or something?"

"Believe me when ah say, honey, you don't want no truck wit no hoodoo. You just leave that snakemoon alone, you hyeh me?"

Riverside Chartres Street, some man and a woman uphold-ing each other in a staggering wedge, they're bouncing off walls; local figure in black called OoooseBadoose, bare-footin otherway, comes off with his trademark pitch, "Oooosebadoose!" (Badoospeak for "Canyousparesome-changeforabitetoeat" so uptempo it came off sounding like "Oooosebadoose!")

Woman said, "Oh my God!" and they passed gone before and footsteps behind . . .

Haste is inharmonious with dimlit antiquity and timeless music.

—Rick Snurd, Napoleon House waiter

Curbside Napoleon House

Lowlit arcaded corner sidewalk, riverside Chartres at St. Louis Street; cornerfront doubledoors giving into a passage in time: relic stucco walls, parquet floors, hyperantique (as in handtrimmed) oak ceilingbeams, lowlying topaz moodlamps (sepia in memory).

Strains of Tannhauser vivid in stereo . . .

Albert Johnson, cornercurbside, looking in on Bob Parker behind the bar at his nazi soul routine: shuteye of reverie morphing into a mock subconscious stiffarm nazi seigheil slowdone dovetailing the Wagner crescendo . . .

At the bar Friggin Bruce and Guru John coming apart.

Albert Johnson subspace *you would probably have to go out of the Quarter to find another place with a dictionary behind the bar*

Shoulder of the bar, Paul Calhoun a headshaking grin: into his shirtpocket a handful of tickets, up with a trayful of drinks—*fuck the napkins*

Round old man in suspenders, Mr. Shep (collar open, bowtie letdown), ponderous at the chesstable, taking an order, turns, not looking, Paul passing in the aisle—Paul's whirlaway balancing act over the beercooler saves a round (slight spills but no dumps); Old Shep being Old Shep: "Ooooh! Ooooh! Watchesef. Watchesef." (Word was Uncle Stadutti had Old Shep covered in his will—job at Napoleon House long as he wanted it, no matter what.)

• • •

Sidestreetside the building Liz Klutch witnessed a man wipe out over a garbage hatch then jump up reflective: "This is a strange place. They lay the dead aboveground and put out their garbage underground. How to figure?"

Liz curbed cart sidedoorway—look in on the kitchen act (streetsweeps in Napoleon House understood uncool except back in the kitchen). Was Mike Ducik, steamtableside, jamming on a sandwich order, and Hobo Jake (true to form random apparel: bush hat, tails, striped tie on a plaid pullover shirt), nodded on a dairycrate, preptableside.

"Mike!"

"Hey."

"You're working."

"All day 'n' all night."

"Howcome?"

"Roy called Sal to come git'im outta jail."

"Are you—what am I saying?—of course you're serious."

"You heard about The House of Abandon got raided."

"Roy?"

"Busted the whole revue, I heard."

"Oh my—hello Jake . . ."

Jake nodded hello and nodded out.

Swinging door giving off Paul Calhoun: bowtie askew, shirttail more out than in, wavy chestnut hair unkept: "Hey babe."

"Hello dear. How're you?"

"Don't ask. *(Onto Liz checking him out)* I'm a case, I know."

"Is it weird in here tonight?"

Mike and Paul heard that.

Paul said, "Job description zookeeper."

Mike said, "And they all axed for you."

Paul said, "Tell me about it."

Liz said, "Full moon, you know."

Mike said, "There it is."

Paul said, "Everybody I've been avoiding all my life has been in here tonight."

Mike said, "Let's talk double jeopardy."

Paul said, "Yeah, really. This guy—"

Liz finished it for him: "Pulling a double, I know."

Mike said, "The supreme sacrifice!" and Paul laughed repeating it.

Liz said, "Poor baby."

Paul said, "You heard about The House of Abandon roundup, I take it."

Liz said, "I heard. Mike just told me about Roy. What a drag."

Paul said, "Drag is right," and Mike agreed, "You got that right."

Paul told Liz, "Roy called Sal, right?"

Liz said, "So I heard."

Paul said, "Wanted'im to get hold of'iz roommate about bringin some clothes."

Liz went, "Oh my . . ."

Mike said, "Do your own figurin."

Liz said, "Really."

Swinging door heralded Bob Parker: "Pardon me, staff," and he cut a sidelong highsign: "This lady needs to find out who her waiter was," and everybody laughed.

Mike said, "Didja get a look at this person?"

Paul said, "No doubt we have a make on the suspect."

The estranged customer, lapful of drinkspill, visibly displeased with the drift, asked Paul, "Were you our waiter?"

Mike said, "Fifth Amendment!" and Paul told her, "Be right with ya," and turned his back—jam some sandwich act.

Indignity of estranged getting estranger: "We've been waiting a long time."

Mike said, "What's that Rick Snurd line? Haste is . . ."

Paul inserted, "Inharmonious—"

Mike continued, "With antiquity—"

Paul inserted, "With *dimlit* antiquity."

Mike took it from the top: "Haste is inharmonious with dimlit antiquity *(now Paul chimed in)* and timeless music."

Bob Parker said, "Absnurdities aside," and Paul laughed repeating, *"Absnurdities!"*

Mike said, "Shouldn't be slobbin down all this food in such a hurry anyway, especially at this hour. Bad for digestion."

Hobo Jake came upface offtabletop, put forth out of nowhere: "People in a hurry make first in the boneyard."

Parker took slack, nodded, "Thank you, I'm sure. The point is there's been an accident at this table. If we could somehow get a mop in the hands of some enterprising busperson with an eye to the future . . ." Perked brow shot Jake, rolling eyes cut Liz, he bailed out the door.

Mike said, "Hear that, Jake? Here's your chance to smoke Rangoon Johnny in the staff promotion sweepstakes!"

Jake was on his feet, he was at Paul's elbow, uplooking in earnest: "Somebody givin you a hard time—I'm comin!"

Paul said, "Truly there is a God."

Mike said, "Looks to me like somebody's wearin the spill."

Paul said, "Chain reaction."

Mike went, "Uh-oh."

Paul said, "See why I consider uptown people tourists?"

The estranged customer had heard enough: "Would someone *mind* telling me where the ladies' room is."

Paul pointed (without looking) directly ahead of her, and Mike said, "Almost found it without askin."

Door squeaking open, the estranged customer stepped aside, enter Old Shep babbling over his orderpad. Contemplating him put slack in her face.

Liz said, "Hello Shep."

Shep jumped up, "*Ooooh!*" People laughed. Shep said, "Oh." He got a grin on: "Haya doin?"

Liz said, "Good, dear. How're you?"

Shep was on the move: "Uh, good, good, unh-hunh." Steamtableside: mug inclined whichways, orderpad thru bifocals; prospects overtop tortoiseshell rims: "Uh, Mike, uh—*ahum*!—these my sandwiches?"

Paul said, "They're mine, Shep, c'mon. Don't be gettin me more scrambled than I am."

(*Jake onto Paul's estranged customer hanging a face on that one*)

Mike said, "You don't have an order up, Shep."

Shep said, "I don't? I don't have one up?"

Mike said, "Not a one, Shep."

Shep took bewildered: "Y'don' ha' no sandwiches fumme?"

Mike said, "What sandwiches, Shep?"

"*Awwwww*, y'don' have'em."

Mike said, "I tolja, Shep, y'didn' put an order up. I can't make sandwiches I don't know about, Shep."

Shep stammered, "Izzat right? I thought I did, I thought I put somp'n up, I thought sure I did."

Mike said, "Think again, Shep."

"*Urngggh* . . ." Slipslide next Paul. "Listen, uh, Paul— wanna take these people? They'll take good care aya."

"Aw, yeah, I'll bet they will, Shep," and Mike said, "Been keepin'em warm just for you!"

Shep said, "Ooooh, they's loaded, man. They got them highclass suits on. Y'know them jackets like Jake has on?"

Paul said, "Keep those penguins, Shep."

"Hep y'out, hepya make some money."

"Give it up, Shep."

Shep got a grin on: "Y'don' want'em?"

"Shep, I got troubles ummy own, I can't be takin you on."

"*Hungggh* . . ." False start, then another. He went out shuffling tickets. "Them otha folks musta paid the wrong bill, mebbe they ate the sandwiches, I dunno . . ."

Paul's estranged customer heard that, she went for the ladies' room.

Jake, all for sitting, seeing her go, stayed afoot.

Mike said, "I'm spozza be a mindreader!"

Paul said, "Kiddin? he'd scramble a mindreader for life."

Liz said, "Be nice, you two."

Reflective grin out Paul: "I come in here on a day off, right? Regular street rags, y'know, t-shirt 'n' jeans. I'm sittin at the chesstable drinkin a beer—Shep comes over: 'Wanna take that party? They'll take good care aya . . .'"

Mike said, "Hey, he comes in tonight, first thing, he's gonna do some fundraising for Jake, right? Comes up to me and goes, 'Jake wants five bucks, and Sal says we hafta give it to'im.'"

Jake didn't even hear that, he was at Paul's elbow: "Somebody give ma buddy a hard time—I'm comin!" Tag wink.

Paul said, "Wear it out, Jake."

Jake said, "Things I can do with a mop a man never seen."

Paul turned to Mike: "That my pastrami?"

Mike said, "You're holdin it."

Paul shook his head, "I'm losin it."

Mike kidded, "Tighten up!"

Frank Pomeroy, the staff ace, leaned in: "Paul, you have a checkout."

Mike said, "Eager to tip, no doubt!" and Liz laughed.

Pomeroy dripping service with a smirk; look cut Liz: "What's happenin?"

"Good question, dear."

Pomeroy said, "Hear about Roy?"

Liz said, "I heard."

Jake passed Pomeroy at the door: ". . . mess wit ma buddy, ahm comin—"

Pomeroy smirked, "Busbum awake finally?"

Liz said, "Don't call him that."

Jake was not out a step: "Pick'em up 'n' lay'em down, ya little bastard."

Mike said, "Ahright Jake!"

Paul said, "Spoken like a true sailor!"

Meantime Jake not taking any bows, no hitch in his getalong, he was out the door and gone.

Pomeroy told Paul, "Your customers are waiting," and turned away, parting shot unclear.

Paul was still laughing, "Pick'em up 'n' lay'em down, ya little bastard . . ." One sandwich act underway.

Liz said, "Make those tips, dear."

Paul said, "Yeah, right."

When Paul was out, Liz said to Mike, "Pretty weird in here, dear."

Mike said, "Tell me about it."

The ladies' room had been happening. Paul's estranged customer came out with another woman sametime Frank Pomeroy was coming in the kitchen and the other woman commenting that their waiter wasn't so bad. The other woman said, "Here he is!" and she cupped Frank's chin and made over him so that he all but blushed. She said to him, "Sweetheart, this dear friend is joining us. Would you be good enough to bring her a drink?"

Frank said, "No problem," and they spirited him out on either arm.

Frank's satisfied customer said to Paul's estranged customer, "Didn't I tell you he's a jewel!" And she snuggled up close: "Well do you know Napoleon House ladiesroom has got to be the best grafitti in town . . ."

Out the door, they hardly noticed Jake, mop at the ready, noticing them.

Albert Johnson stepped in the door with a glovetiphold on a cigar butt he had found: Mike motioned an ashtray, preptabletop; Albert did the drop.

Mike said, "Jake thanks you, I'm sure."

Albert said, "A foolproof assumption."

Herecome Paul: "Albert. Hey."

Albert grinned at Paul: "Quite the acrobatic rescue of your tray out there moments ago. (*Paul looking wha?*) The little slapstick with your senior colleague by the chesstable . . ."

Paul said, "Oh. You caught that, uh?"

Albert grinned, "Between you and Bob Parker this place is the hottest ticket in town tonight."

Mike asked Albert, "Speakin of Parker being hot, does he know you're here?"

Paul grinned, "Please."

Mike said, "Anything but Parker in heat."

Paul said, "Really. I mean, hey, y'know? Give us a break."

Liz said, "I love Bob."

Paul was on his way out with more sandwichplates: "Slapstick with my senior colleague . . ."

Liz told Albert, "Mike's filling in while Roy's a guest of the DA."

Albert said, "Roy made The House of Abandon convocation?"

Mike said, "Spitshine busted in progress rate blotter fodder?"

Albert said, "I rather assumed harrassment charges weren't simply a matter of the raid happening at showtime."

Mike said, "Rumor has it when somebody was apprehended People's Exhibit A was still standing."

Albert said, "I could feature singing sisters in a plea bargain on that one."

Mike said, "There it is. Another vice rap goes away for a song."

Herecome Frank Pomeroy: "Hey. What's happenin?"

Albert said, "This place is happening."

Frank said, "Happenin down, maybe." He was up with a food order. "I can't believe Paul, man. Customer requests Mozart, right? Paul goes, Jupiter Symphony all right? Customer says sure. Paul goes, It's been on for five minutes, and walks away."

Liz said, "For heavensake."

Mike said, "I love it!"

Albert said, "Paul is perfecting the fine art of getting people compensating from the wallet."

Frank said, "That what he's doing?" He was walking on that. "Later."

Mike laughed: "It's been on for five minutes . . ."

Liz shook her head: "That's too much."

Shep was coming in the door—voice called across the room: "Hey Shep!"

Shep went, "Ooooh! yesyesyes," he was turning back out the door: "Okayokayokay . . ."

Sniff out Mike, he shook his head: "Come on two o'clock."

Liz said, "Poor dear. You must be exhausted."

Paul came busting in: "I'm losin it. I mean I'm about to . . . I dunno what I'm about to . . ."

Liz said, "Calm down, dear."

Paul said, "Phone's ringin off the hook, right? Parker's flyin, he can't get to it. Customers callin out answer the phone. Finally about the umpteenth ring I pick it up—voice on the line goes, 'Can you hold on a second?'"

Mike said, "No!" Motion slam.

Paul said, "Yeah, really." He sparked a smoke and pulled. "Could I hold on a second . . ."

Jake shuffled in, got next Paul. He just did get it out: "Turned yer table fuyya."

Paul said, "Well that's good news. Is that good news?"

Mike said, "Kill the messenger anyway."

Paul laughed: "Yeah, right."

Jake had more to tell, just couldn't bring it; lost it in a bellylaugh instead.

Paul grinned smoke: "Wear it out, Jake."

Frank busted in wanting godawful bad in Jake's face: "The fuck is your problem?"

Paul hung coverage: "Hey, ease up."

Frank said, "I'll ease up."

(*Jake, sudden lookout, something blunt for grabhold, eyeballed the cigar butt, scooped it instead.*)

Paul said, "What's comin off?"

Frank said, "I'll tellya what's comin off. This asshole just ran my eighttop and half my station with it." (*Jake jumped up bad, "Hey!" sunk retrobad, coughing, same breath*) Frank was on his way out: "This will get back to Sal, I promise you that. This situation can't go on. He's costing this place money."

Paul went out after Frank, and Mike after Paul. Shep could be heard out the door speaking to Frank, but his voice trailed off unlistened to. Shep came in daubbing his eyes.

Liz said, "Shep, what on *earth* is going on out there?"

Shep went, "*Urngggggh*—Jake jess mopped in Frank's room. It was a whole big bottle of ammonia in 'at bucket. I said, Hyeee, Jake, whattaya doin? He said, Nevayoumine what ahm doin. Jake gets like 'at. Jake drinks, y'know. Jake drinks too much."

Jake was getting to his feet.

Mike came in: "Jake, I think you just wrotecher ticket outta here, buddy."

Jake said, "I don't give a damn. I don't need this place."

Mike made with a highsign by Jake: "Did a white cloud number on Frank's station."

Liz said, "We heard."

Shep said, "Frank is mad, baw, he's mad, Frank is real mad."

Jake said, "Aw quitcher yappin, you shitface ole bitty."

Shep went, "Ooooh!" hushing motion, looksee who was hearing.

Liz said, "Be nice, now, Jake."

Shep said, "It's a lady present, Jake."

Jake said, "I know it is."

Shep said, "C'mon now, act right."

Paul blew in: "*Jeee*-sus Christ, Jake." Face to face with Jake, he could only go long on the outbreath, he just shook his head.

Mike said, "Hey, y'know what? Some hurtin public relations style went down, but the man's intentions were right on—maybe even righteous."

Paul nodded, "What can I say? Right people, wrong room."

Frank came in, went straight to Paul: "Some of my customers are joining your party at 4b. They want me to wait on'em."

Paul said, "Fine, no argument." He pulled his tickets, pulled 4b.

Frank was saying, "That spill still needs to be mopped, and that's on you and not him."

Paul forked over the ticket: "Take those losers."

Fortified smile out Frank: "This is even up, now. Don't be tellin me I owe you any parties."

Paul said, "Tellya what." He tossed live tickets prep-tabletop. "Howbout you pull the whole show, howzat?"

Frank mug *wha?*

Parker came singsong in the door: "*Wait*-ers . . . *Check*-outs . . . Better get out here while they're willing to *pa-aaaaay* . . ."

Frank and Shep made the door for their stations; Paul the door to the street.

Parker said, "Where, dare I ask, might you be going?"

Paul said, "Wherever pickin'em up 'n' layin'em down takes me," and was last heard outside and upstreet.

Parker, deadpan, noticing Albert, got a face: "Albert!"

Albert beamed Parker a givinghand finger rub.

Parker said, "Do you be*lie*ve what I'm up against here? One waiter gone; another not all here. Feature waiter with a personality about an inch and a half long. Our sandwich chef is in Parish Prison in pantyhose and pumps. Busperson out of Baptist Mission driving away customers. What to make of all this?"

Albert shrugged, "Service St. Jude would stiff is one of the unlikely charms of this place."

Parker got a face on: "Thank you, Albert. You'd be unforgettable at a wake."

Liz brought Bob a big hug.

Jake down preptableside, liplock on the stogie: Mike flicked bic sparking him.

Outlaw on a chopped hog bombing wrongway up Orleans Street. Nellie queen, curbside, foursquare in a crotchrocket stance, makes with a television cartoon jingle: *"Go speed ra-cer / Go speed ra-cer / Go speed racer, Go-ooooo . . ."*

Place called The Grog. Dyke warren upto Rampart at Orleans:

. . . backstage window over Dom Dominique's, otherside Orleans Street: boys getting in and out dresses and lingerie;

. . . oneway door at hand, faint thru the mirror image: lowlight of moodlamps back of the bar . . .

The dude could buzz in The Grog came connected. Johnny Albesharpe and the barkeep, Tasha, were neighbors. Johnny buzzed in and cut straight to the bathroom.

Moments later Shushubaby buzzed in on the scene.

Place was jamming; soundsystem banging, wall-to-wall bump and grind—heads back, fists pumping, gutbucket singalong refrains. (Marylyn Rue, selfproclaimed pile-drivingest bulldyke on Rampart Street, backroom between pooltables, looming on a chair: hyperraunchy lipsynch, fretburning airguitar.)

Shushubaby and Tasha were chatting, Johnny showed lighter from the bathroom.

Shushubaby chided him, "Couldn't wait, uh?" and Tasha said, "Or say hi even?"

Johnny said, "I had the hershey squirts from that soul-food over Myrti's."

While Shushubaby cooled off at the bar, Johnny found soul rivalry at pinball. Fellow silverball freak in bowtie, vest and derby name of Lydia. Play lit up a tilt apiece.

Rubbermatch gameball he put a sporting caress on her; she shimmied up the embrace. They wound up dancing off the tune that was playing. Not appreciated all corners. Magnum butch in a Rebel Yell t-shirt, shouldering thru the boogeying throng, jumped up toe-to-toe with Johnny, elbows back. Johnny got this grin: "It's cool, it's cool." Got put knowing different—grabhold knucklebuckle put on his thumb made Johnny yelp. The torpedo hustled Lydia off the dancefloor while Johnny stood flatfooted nursing his thumb and hellhouse rocking out to funky music rocked on. Enough not happening on a happening dancefloor, he retroboogied a backdoor retreat.

Shushubaby found him brooding curbside.

"What wuzzat about?"

"Fuckin hammerhead dyke, man. Puts her butch in my face. I tried to mellow'er out 'n' got fuckin bent. Totally uncalled for, man. Pissed me off."

Place like Barranco's you could get your feelings hurt

Intense bar up St. Philip Street. You had to know where the place was at. Doubledoors inviting mistake for a sidestreetside delivery entrance of the corner grocery nextdoor. Overhead sign longtime hungdown broke. Close quarters windowless except behind the bar (jerryrigged airconditioner run on faith—hurting for cool but it did blow). Myth had a fire marshall and health inspector tripping each other up in a rush to shut the place down.

Quadrophonic bangin to burn. Louise Broussard (Shushubaby's sister) dancing in a scatterspace, hands overhead, plenty would-be grind in those hips—kind of a hybrid spanish flamingo/philly dog attempt. Some guy in a chair stroking roundhouse handjive in appreciation; Louise tittering, "You sonuvabitch!"

Art Nieman and Brooklyn Bob were hanging out with Mary Mosley (late of Haight-Ashbury and Woodstock; claim to fame was busting Jimi Hendrix and Janis Joplin fucking in a Fillmore West toilet).

Mary saw Bev and Milo coming in: "Hey guys!"

Milo nodded: "Citizens."

Brooklyn Bob said, "We're drinking to Newberry compliments of Newberry."

Milo hung *wha?*

Brooklyn Bob said, "He won the pool. Newberry won the pool."

Milo beetled: "*New*berry?"

Brooklyn Bob nodded, "Weird, uh?"

Milo hung with the notion: "Newberry won the pool . . . "

Brooklyn Bob said, "Called the winner dead on—no pun intended."

Bev said, "Far be it from you to be insensitive."

Brooklyn Bob said, "Do I hear a prospect for the loyal opposition?"

Mary Mosley said, "Pack the editorial comments, Bob."

Brooklyn Bob motioned sidelong by Mary: "Morally outraged at the idea of an open bar outta Newberry's jackpot—as if Newberry wouldna been down with it."

Mary said, "That's not the point, Bob."

Brooklyn Bob said, "Wants we should roll the pot over to next week's pool."

Mary said, "Listen to you coming off like a midway pitchman, Bob."

Brooklyn Bob said, "In other words somebody walks with Newberry's take and then some."

Mary said, "Somebody slow to stand drinks, for instance?"

Brooklyn Bob said, "Can we withhold judgment here, Mary?"

"Manipulation is what needs to be withheld here."

"We can't withhold judgment."

"Oh c'mon, Bob. Any fool can see who's drinking Newberry's memory and who's just drinking the giveaway, I mean let's face it."

"Hey, the money's put up in good faith, okay? That much is straight. How people spend it is on them not us."

"Granted—"

"Thank you."

"Intentions are in the right place—"

"I rest my case."

"All I'm saying, Bob, is the freeloading going on here is way outta proportion to any friends Newberry ever had around here. How that honors anybody's memory is lost on me, I'm sorry."

Louise Broussard had danced her way tableside, she came in with jezebel affect: "Awww, y'all commisseratin about Newberreh?"

Brooklyn Bob raised his glass: "To a beautiful loser."

Mary said, "Bounce that one all the way up, Bob."

Louise said, "Ah am *shocked*!"

Brooklyn Bob said, "C'mon, we're all losers. That's what we're doin in a bar."

Louise took exception: "Wha the *ve*reh ef-*fron*tereh!"

Mary said, "Bob, you're such an asshole sometimes. I hate it when you talk like that."

Brooklyn Bob said, "Hey, if it's my character you're questioning, Mary, I resent your tone of voice."

Mary said, "You sound like Dickinthedirt."

Brooklyn Bob made doubled over with this lowblow to the kingship aftergasp: *"That remark came in with pointed boots, Mary—goddamn."* He was down on some lowblow contractions for effect.

Mary said, "You've made your point, Bob."

Bev spoke in Mary's ear, "Before I go, may I buy you a drink?" and Mary had to laugh.

Sometimes you had to be ready for this place. Bev split round the corner—get down on some street medicine:

. . . moonlit housefront: twostory, unpainted; lamplit silhouette peeking thru louvers . . .

. . . *Sidewalks of plenty to be cruised and cruised again:*

'56 T-bird rolls by . . .

Couple queens strolling upstreet, walkingcups in hand—prissy giggles, hushed hissing tones.

T-bird swings another pass; pulls longside . . .

One got in.

The other threw down his cup and walked . . .

Mary joined Bev curbside.

"Lotta moon on these streets."

"Really."

"Thanks again for the drink, hon."

"Viva opposition solidarity."

"That Bob."

"He is a trip."

"Let me ask you something, Bev. Would you know if Shushubaby has seen Alvin Lee recently?"

"I wouldn't know."

"The reason I ask, I heard this rumor about Alvin. In fact, it's so outlandish I probably shouldn't repeat it."

"Alvin rumor—outlandish?"

"I know. Anyway—between you and me and the lamppost . . ."

"In the vault."

"Okay. You know Pamela Hardesty who comes in here?"

"Tight tanktops."

"You're aware she's married to the assistant coroner."

"Aware enough to know you'd never know."

"Well it may be he's found out about Alvin Lee."

"Doesn't surprise me."

"Rumor has it Pamela got Alvin's cock in the mail."

Crosslooks *heard what I heard?* Answered *you heard.*

"That sounds a bit suspicious to me."

"No sooner I tell myself it's only a hoax it occurs to me what if it isn't."

"Postal service, that's federal heat, you know."

"Special delivery in a laboratory specimen jar."

"I'd have to see the exhibit. I'm hard pressed to fathom even somebody just making that up."

"Well nobody's seen them around lately Alvin or Pamela either one is the thing. Although I have heard that Pamela might be at her mom's over in Biloxi."

"If you ask me this cock in the specimen jar here and gone the way of the moon would be about the only special delivery I could make of all this."

Meantime Milo called Charity Emergency for word on the Bourbon Street Takee Outee case. Subject listed stable for all but dodging a bullet at pointblank range. Slug leftside lovehandle, fleshwound thru and thru, bloodloss nonthreatening. Probable discharge pending precautionary overnight observation.

Milo brought the news.

Mary trumped it.

Milo had already heard. He said, "Y'know, with all this birthplace of jazz hype you get around here, people overlook this is also the birthplace of Jim Crow. Even so, brother cock Special D to a faithless lady, I'd say that's a little weird even for this place."

Bev said, "Makes you wonder where a thing like that comes from."

Milo said, "Some vigilante rank advocate got a figment on, I reckon."

Bev said, "Leaves off anything I've heard in a while."

Mary said, "Personally, I'm not satisfied it's a hoax till I see Alvin—not that I'm ready, even then, to go by anything he tells me."

Bev said, "Feature Alvin with a white woman ending the hoax where it began."

Forbert made a pit stop in Molly's on Toulouse. Offed covershade stood acts in uncut light. Stopped up toilet, sticky floor, Black Sabbath muffled thru the firewall (Dungeon nextdoor) . . . Offcolor trace of a wallhanging hung no more, annex of new inspiration to ease bladders by: this lead entry writ fountain blue: *"The only good man was Jesus Christ."* Next that, in bold red flare, lettered to perfection, earmarks of a stickler for details: *"Why callest thou me good? There is none good but One, that is, God." —Matthew 19:17*. Under these, in fine blue ballpoint, a less exacting hand: *"There's one in every crowd."* Then some song and dance revisionist in blackflare: *"Christ may, or may not, have been the original hippie, but who, if not Him, was the forerunner of surfing?"* Bottomline, in dull pencilpoint, complete with accompanying sketch, somebody's drummer: *"I'm so horny the crack of dawn isn't safe."*

Out on the street, curbside Funky Butts, was a rumble in the making over bad shit somebody put down about Harley Davidson.

• • •

Leo and Doc waited Forbert on the truck.

"Dink ath real, podna? Unh? Dink ath real? Ahm a long time been rounna Quatuth, podna, don' nuttin git ba me, umma teyya . . . Lookadat. Look. Fool can't tell, podna. You belieb at? He dink ath furreal. Lookadat fool. Talkin at talk lok itha poke gonna git got. Dink momma done tole him bot dem kon lok da one marrid dad only makebelieve? Paw fool he in fa thum konna thaproth! *(Footlong handjive, gutbucketbust of a laugh)* Dink ahm kiddin? Whaf hangin neef at thkoit probla bigga'n what ah got in ma panth! You dink ahm kiddin? Probla bigga peta on him'n' ah got, he don' want it, he want mine! Atha trufe, podna, betta belieb it. Itha trufe lok ahm tellinya. Ahm not gonna la t'ya, podna, umma teyya true. Ah don' got a big peta, ah got a little bitty peta."

. . . Sugar Bowl weekend, specter of Alabama faithful on the Quarter; Leo took exception to some kid hopping sideboard—"Da hellya dink ya doin?" Kid snatched his hat (got his hairpiece with it)—made off down Bourbon Street. The rug turned up out Blaha's route, but the lid never did get recovered. Hear Doc tell it, Leo hadn't been the same truckdriver since . . .

Was brokenfield stickwork Hidden Dave and Shushubaby got shootin down midway Bourbon Street. Meantime Albesharpe and United Cab Ronnie ponied up party sacrament Natalie and Ramone could keep good heads on. After that deal went down they came got Shushubaby. Hidden Dave took a pass on headship invites, he was locked into mule consciousness: get Bourbon Street got, if even singlehanded—down lakeside, back riverside—trademark *inspired shootin stick.*

Sheathed in sweat and that in moonlight was some way to be.

Weedlot wayside Conti Street: stairway upside bare buildingside; no windows, no doors, head or foot the stairs: nowhere to nowhere else up or down. Sensitive vistas of The Meat Hook and The House of Abandon. Narcopolis of choice one stairway to headship.

United Cab Ronnie was saying: "Fuckin House of Abandon, man. Once carried the same dude three fares same night—different trick every time."

Albesharpe said, "Could be a hack record."

United Cab Ronnie said, "Manifest in highlighter was a week on the dispatcher's wall, man, I shitchu not."

Albesharpe said, "Man, you shoulda seen Dom Dominique's tonight."

Shushubaby said, "Really. It was like a Fellini movie in there."

Albesharpe said, "They got this strobe on the stairway, right. It's like this gauntlet of dicks up the stairway, man, I mean it was unreal. Some dude's gettin fistfucked on the banister, y'know. It was outta control."

United Cab Ronnie hung retro: "Reminds me one night, pouring rain, I get this middle age queen outta Dom's for this submeter symphony fare all the way across Rampart Street, right? Whole time he's raggin on the bar scene, y'know: 'I don't need those hussies. Some of the best sexual experiences I've ever had were jerkin off.' Even money on the fare, right. No tip. He's tellin me be nice and pull closer to the curb. He's got expensive shoes on, right, he doesn't wanna get'em wet."

Shushubaby had to laugh: "Oh no!"

Albesharpe shook his head: "Fuckin ream, man."

United Cab Ronnie said, "I shoulda asked if jerkin off insteada payin for it is how an overthehill stiff affords expensive shoes."

Albesharpe said, "Or how would his lovelife withstand the sorta karma he was bringin on the proverbial giving hand!" (*Staccato cackle*)

United Cab Ronnie said, "The implifuckincation I'm an asshole is what I didn't care for."

Shushubaby said, "Oh don't be silly. People're gonna have their trips. Be glad it wasn't a long ride."

United Cab Ronnie said, "By the way, I passed by La Casa earlier. The Babaloo Indians got Jivin Jeff Dean blowin harp again. So what's with Alvin Lee?"

Shushubaby said, "I don't know. What I heard was Alvin didn't show up for a demo recording or whatever so Huey Noyes kicked'im outta the band."

Albesharpe said, "Hear Alvin tell it, Huey has no time for anybody's creative input but his own."

Shushubaby said, "Huey's just jealous cuz Alvin gets all the chicks."

Streetscape:

Curbside The House of Abandon: leather number manhandling some Bowie clone by the collar—took his man across the mug these backhand/forehand combination cuffs:

Forehand/backhand/forehand: "Admit you're a ripoff motherfucker."

"Take your hands off of me, you fucking goon."

Forehand/backhand/forehand: "Admit you're a ripoff motherfucker."

"Goddamn you to hell, unhand me, I insist."

Thirdparty coverage (piedmont accent): "Is this necessary?"

United Cab Ronnie said, "Two hundred years ago that wudda been somebody's life in a duel down Exchange Alley. Fuckin don't laugh, I'm fuckin serious, man. This city was about opera before it was about jazz."

Albesharpe hung retro: "Other night these two dudes come flyin outta there, man, dude makes a flyin tackle in the street, he's poundin the shit outta the dude, man: '*I love you, goddammit, I love you, I love you*'—he's poundin the dude into the street, man."

Shushubaby said, "Both dudes probably diggin it."

United Cab Ronnie said, "It's a wonder some visionary hustler hasn't hit on some kinda lowlife tour package of the French Quarter yet. Y'know, kinduva downtown answer to guided swamp tours. I mean stone outlaw guides, man—we're talkin lowlife tours of the backstreets and underground warrens of the Quarter."

Albesharpe said, "Lowlife Voyeurs, Unlimited."

United Cab Ronnie said, "Hang that shingle! Be a welcome contrast to all the prefabricated funk gettin trafficked around here anymore, if you ask me. I mean it's like this place is gettin to be some kinda themepark for corporate industrial androids on liberty, man. All the blueblood 'n' graduate types you see doin The 'Dip—'n' that's their idea of slummin. Fuckin Beanwagon, man, that place is a glorified Luckydog Cart, almost by definition. Just peekin in some doors around here can make you feel like some kinda philistines rights advocate anymore. I foresee French Quarter character impersonators hired to amuse american squares."

Albesharpe said, "Yeah: Some Ruthie the Ducklady impersonator working Dugan's Beanwagon. OoooseBadoose at the Blue Room."

United Cab Ronnie said, "Hey, y'know Milo's heard tell of five figure federal bread ponied up for some sorta documentary on the vanishing roadside diner. Man, if somethin like that gets over, I mean you gotta know the vanishing Quarter funkscape is anthropology whose time has come."

. . . Pre G-Man Elvis out some jukebox some joint upstreet . . .

Three sales reps suit attack Pirates Alley, direction Jackson Square; Fried Jimmy McBride coming off the plaza cut them a gaptooth grin: "Got somethin for ya!"—comes out his pocket with pennies at their feet . . .

Toulouse Street

Hidden Dave curbed cart outside Funky Butts—wide berth cut the Luckydog Cart cornerside, Harley hogs otherside (health considerations both ways).

Shushubaby found him in Molly's in a barberchair getting down on sounds. Got this look about him.

"What're you grinning about?"

"Just thinkin about Proffit tellin Tommy one more fuckup 'n' he better be streetwise."

"Those two're a trip."

"A show to set watches by."

"Really."

"Proffit gets bored he resorts to Tommy for entertainment."

"You think Bobo's witty?"

"Yeah. I do."

"I've been meaning to ask somebody intelligent if Bobo's witty."

"Whattayou think?"

"Me? I dunno. I'm not one of those intellectual types, y'know. I can't tell if he's witty or a smartass."

"Intelligent inquiry."

"Sweet of you to lie."

"Not at all. Probably alotta hip snobbery on the subject.

Shitbottom truth of the matter is Albert Johnson's about the only one I've seen cover Proffit deep in a match of wits."

"I love Albert."

"Albert Johnson is the most elegant person I know."

"Can't argue with that."

(Hidden Dave with his way of looking like he knew your last sin)

Shushubaby said, "What?"

Hidden Dave said, "You're a thinking stiff's cure."

"Whatever that is."

"You know what you know."

"Whatever that means."

"You think with your heart."

"Dave, you're such a bullshitter. I love it."

Place called Nellie's upto Rampart Street. Pabst on tap, Dixie down the well; jukebox true country (when a two by four was two by four).

"What's the good word, Bobo?"

"Wouldn't tellya if ah knew."

"Wouldn't believe ya if ya did."

"You tight all night, Nell. Evabody knozzat."

"Them hippiz draggin you in they downdraft, Bobo?"

"Get dis. Now hippiz say hippiz ain' hippiz no more. They ex-hippiz now, see."

"Sound to me like somebody's dauber's in the dirt."

"You know it too?"

"Them hippiz somp'n else, Bobo."

"Hippiz alwiz been somp'n else, ah got news fuyya. Dat's howcome hippiz wuz hippiz to begin wit."

"Now they wanna be somp'n else again fa Godsake."

"Ain't dat somp'n? Now dey claimin newpapiz 'n' television got hippiz all wrong, see. So it was some makebelieve funeral yeaz ago ott'n San Francisco laid away this so called real hippie newspapiz 'n' television got all wrong. Dat's how come they ex-hippiz anymore, see, on accounnadat funeral."

"Now that would be one funeral I'll bet I could second-line."

"Well it wuz makebelieve is the thing, see. Wudn' no real soul, unnestan, just some dummy wit long hair 'n' hip-pie clothes on."

"Sounds hippie enough for me to bury, Bobo."

"What ah tell'em, ah say, What abot Chawles Manson? Wudn' he papa hippie? Chawles Manson still aroun, ain' he? Don' make me no diffence Chawles Manson inside. Chawles Manson still aroun all hippiz ain' gone, simple azzat. Dey can roll 'at in they zigzags 'n' nevamind, 'at's what ah tell'em."

"Don't nobody wanna bring me nunnadat bulltweed they don't want they feelins huyt."

"You a hawd bidnesswoman, Nell."

He brings me this drawing Doc done of some dogheaded man he
wants I should tattoo. Names me some name some god he says
took souls to the afterlife. Ask me wuzzat too spooky to ask. I
says to the man I says, Don't make a shit to me none. Well, sir,
he laidiz money down, and the dogheaded man he wanted was
the dogheaded man he got. Well I dunno wuz he alla
twentyfour hours gone outta here I got Joe Bananas in here
tellin me alcohol poisonin done the man in. Now they're all
upto Barranco's drinkin off that prizemoney he'll never know
he won in that pool they got on? Be goddamned do I even know
what I wonder about somebody goes out like that.

—Tex Rowe

Rampart Street slavequarter

Tex Rowe was an outlier out of Texas, status no looking
back (story was Tex paid off penitentiary time—cold trail
off the range to the bargain).

A happening tattoo practice afforded cover of whatever
else went on at this place. Lone adornment on walls of
exposed bargeboard this ink drawing by Doc showing Mt.
Rushmore fivestrong with Alfred E. Neuman. Folks of all
description from all directions showed up at all hours looking
for Tex.

A haunt of irretrievables never was if not here. Ooose-
Badoose frequented; likewise The Beadlady and Ruthie the
Ducklady (both sporting complimentary tattoos). Fried
Jimmy McBride called it halfway house. Joe Bananas came
to throw dice (cockfights were rumored but unconfirmed).
Vernon Dickinthedirt Rappaport would testify till Tex
called time for choir practice. Streetsweeps came and went.
Taxis cleared and carried offmeter.

Tex cut a sawedoff Buffalo Bill look, hair down, face long, impressariol air. Hear him tell it, only way he stayed alive in this world he was eightysixed in Hell. (It was said of Tex he could cut bargains with the Devil and cut bargains with the Lord and doublecross Both and break away clean every time.) Consensus hustler's apprentice Max Tron stood living proof Tex Rowe knew his way round the land of bilk and money. The neon gameboard Max Tron put on the street with showcock Deacon John went electric with an old sideshow dodge Tex cut Max in on. By the moon a bantam rooster was a monster on Bourbon Street.

Tex was saying, "Three times he laidiz money down! You don't think he was grandstandin? You can't tell me he wadn' tryna clue the crowd to a fix."

Paul Calhoun late of Napoleon House say, "Hey, his money's down, he sets himself up as a shill, use'im."

Tex said, "Yeah, well before he matches wits with a chicken in public he wants he can see the pinball he can walk away from without he gets hisself jacked up by some dieseldyke got the red ass on'im."

Albert Johnson said, "To the pinball wars in a genuine Deacon John t-shirt!"

Tex howled.

Albert said, "Collector's issue, of course."

Tex said, "Damn you to hell, Albert—ahm not even mad anymore!"

OoooBadoose was a dark man of Persian extraction who walked the streets barefoot in black. Namesake of his own hallmark panhandling pitch (typically shined on for sheer nonsense), wonder was the man ever ate, though hearsay held he could get it said (unusual suspect for The Royal Street Sage bylines of *The NOLA Express* and occasionally *Figaro*, plus letter to the editor action in *The Times Picayune*). Tex Rowe looked on OoooBadoose perplexed was he bughouse or onto something.

Herecome Hidden Dave and Shushubaby.

Tex said, "What's goin on?"

Hidden Dave said, "Whole lotta moon goin on."

Liz Klutch said, "Happy snakemoon, dear."

Tex said, "What I wanna know is what's so snake about a moon called snakemoon? That's what I wanna know."

OoooBadoose spoke up: "On rare occasions when planetary bearings make like a snake on a plane of the sun the presiding moon is known as snakemoon."

Tex Rowe perked brow: "Either I'm not trackin too close or one of us is shittin upstream."

Liz said, "I just assumed snakemoon was some sort of swamp culture thing or something, y'know?"

OoooBadoose said, "I'll tell you this. People pro snake on Genesis have got to be feeling good about now."

Tex said, "So what's the occasion? Doomsday? Kingdom Come?"

OoooBadoose said, "Pilgrimage of the twiceborn west to Eden."

Hidden Dave nodded, "*West* to Eden—I like that."

Albert Johnson said, "Behold a holy sequel in the stars!"

OoooseBadoose said, "The true story begins where the known story ends."

Tex said, "Yeah, well I'm once dead east of Texas, you're tellin me I can roll over twiceborn west to Eden, that deal goes down, I mean citytime."

OoooseBadoose said, "Picture Lord of Eden reborn a daughter of Eve."

Albert Johnson nodded, "Some topspin on the Wheel of Karma with that development."

OoooseBadoose said, "Forbidden fruit carryover. Realize what I'm saying. Lord of Eden mixes in the operations of nature. This is not Eternal Spirit, this is a lesser god and a jealous one. This lord is a glorified bagman shipping karma (subject to karma as the next soul at that)."

Albert said, "Perhaps inspiration whose time has come."

Hidden Dave said, "Come time called endtime perhaps."

Tex said, "Y'know by God I dunno but what this daughter of Eve gal you mention done been 'n' I'm known'er."

United Cab Ronnie said, "Which wife wuzzat, Tex?"

Albert said, "And did you or did you not deliberately miss the apple on her head?"

Liz told them, "Behave yourselves."

Tex said, "Not my mother's son."

OoooseBadoose told Tex, "If this person put hands on the sick and picked up snakes chances are this person was a daughter of Eve in the flesh."

Tex had to laugh, "Hell, Doose, I'm alla seven times married to women could do that for Godsake. Ain't been the first time divorced neither, if you wanna know 'n' won't never tell."

Liz said, "You're awful."

Albert beetled, "Actually, wouldn't marrying the erst-while Lord of Eden reborn a daughter of Eve make your mother's son Lord of Eden by marriage?"

Liz went, "Oh my God . . ."

Hidden Dave said, "I'm still catchin up to the notion of the Lord of Eden reborn a daughter of Eve."

Liz said, "I love it!"

Shushubaby said, "Daughter of Eve. That's cute."

Albert said, "A Mardi Gras conceit for the ages."

OooseBadoose said, "Figurative momentum and then some with this moon of moons. No wonder this holocination I'm having is happening. Object proof symbols deploy nonverbal intelligence (and nonverbal intelligence deconstructs memory). You figure divine memory is the seed of the dreamfield, and myth is dream writ transpersonal, dreamscape Eden is hallowed by its figurative momentum. In the round hidden meanings lost on the ages are divined by holocination. The rivers of Eden reflect Holy Om. Adam and Eve signify the dual currents of experience. The snake evokes evolutionary current, and the Lord of Eden represents Ego. The Tree of Knowledge stands for Intelligence, and conscience in rays of pure reason are its fruits. The Tree of Life is Divine Memory (duly witnessed in tranquility, the ability to see truth). All told, the forbidden fruit shakedown is a soulbust metaphor. The Tree of Life disinheritance evokes Divine Memory lapse phasing in world appearance, and exile from Eden is the illusion of separation. In the balance, East Eden is the pivotal symbol, East Eden windows the worlds: outward one seeming many; inward all as one. On one level, frontier east represents sleight of force foreshadowing world appearance, morph atomic shell. On another level, frontier east represents the frontal lobe of the brain, and the cherubs posted there shift wise to hemispheres of the neocortex. As for the flaming sword turning all directions, this, of course, evokes Divine Eye, the self illumination of the twiceborn, seeing all before and behind."

Albert said, "You've given this some thought."

OooseBadoose nodded: "I see fruit on snakeslough offered at the Tree of Life. I see The Savior howling in dreamscape Eden: *'Blessed is he who stands at the Beginning, for he understands the end without suffering death.'*"

United Cab Ronnie dropped Liz off by her place down Decatur Street.

Liz walked blind into a happening bathroom. Here was Buford Horseman, her houseguest out of Texas, tricked out in a Beaux Arts ball gown: drinking glass for an earhorn, eavesdropping thru the wall: nextdoor Tommy Blaha barking like a hound dog; some pillowpounding chicken number moaning, "Oh wolf, wolf, oh wolf . . ." Buford all of hundredtwentyweight at sixfootsix in outsize mock tulle, downsouth frontage waxing earnest, grinding against the wall. Found out, he bolted, split out the room—longshot disclaimer the drinking glass ditched in dirty laundry. Liz went upside the wall with the drinking glass, get in some eavesdropping of her own. Special effects no tipoff who was Tommy's pony, she gave it up, put up the cup, go see about Buford.

Next room, she came in on Buford down to his briefs, gown at his feet, riffling thru a press, muttering, "Jesus *Christ* this is humiliating—*shit.*"

Liz said, "I don't believe it."

Buford started: "I would prefer this hadn't happened."

"A chifforobe full of choices and you put on a Beaux Arts ball gown."

"Sheer frolic, I might point out."

"Well, dear, you could do worse than an understated boner in overstated drag, I suppose."

"That's not productive."

"Buford, why don't you come along to the moonswoon at the square? Some social contact would do you some good. You look like you're hearing echoes or something."

"All your friends are gay."

"You're a long way from Grand Prairie, dear."

"I'm perplexed. I'm very perplexed."

"Don't be perplexed."

"Which would you say was inconsistent, my characterization of your friends being gay or the alleged, quote/unquote, understated boner in overstated drag, which would you say?"

"Quote/unquote, alleged?"

"I would prefer not to be ridiculed."

"Which made you feel more alive? Buford, you tell me."

Buford hung it hangdog: "Who's gonna be there?"

Hidden Dave and Shushubaby walking down Orleans Street—straightaway moonspect backside of St. Louis Cathedral foot of Orleans at Royal Street:

"Dave, you're really handsome, but I think I'll pass on you as a lover and just keep you as a friend."

(*Giggle with a blush over his mug surprise*)

"Am I giving off some kinduva scent or something?"

"You silly thing!"

"*What brought that on?*"

"I don't know. I just like to be upfront with people."

"Upfront with people! I'll say you're upfront with people. Like the Nazi Blitzkrieg was upfront with people!"

"You're a trip."

III

West to Eden

... It was gonna happen then it wasn't gonna happen then it just happened. Not like anybody made it happen, necessarily, it all just sorta came together on the pulse somehow. Thing is now you get all these differing versions what happened, y'know, or how it happened, even if it happened. Some things not everybody is sure about, then again some people aren't sure about anything. Guess you might say it was one of those things . . .

—George Forbert

Somebody flipped a killswitch.

—Tommy Blaha

It remains open to question was this blackout down Jackson Square manmade or else. Eyewitness accounts of a utility truck parked on Decatur Street cannot be officially confirmed. No service order exists on file, nor were any utility workers identified in the area, nor any operations observed . . . There at dusk, gone at dawn, seen by no one coming or going, this mystery truck endures in underground skullduggery. Suspicion persists that some who saw the truck may have sworn they did not, and some who did not may have sworn that they did (among whom some, moreover, may have changed their minds) . . . Public utility should possess trucks numerous as stories told about this one.

—*Who Turned Out The Lights?*
by The Royal Street Sage
NOLA Express

When the lights went out on the square, people just assumed Max Tron had done his thing. Well, I've known Max Tron a long time. Me 'n' Max Tron go back to the old days of Seventh House Co-Op over on Royal Street. The thing about Seventh House, they had these three fires, two while I was there and the other when I was on the way. Well Max Tron, he was like this resident technical wizard at Seventh House, he did all their wiring and rewiring and so forth there . . . So you get the idea why Max Tron annointed peoples' choice to stage a moonswoon wouldn't exactly be my call to moonboots. Anyway, all that aside, it turns out Max Tron thought the full moon was the following night, that's when he put his move on—and didn't get it done then—so he could only make good for nothin afterall. In any event, what nobody seems to know, or somebody isn't telling, is how those lights at the square actually did go out, and right on max at that . . .

—Brooklyn Bob Ravenscroft

. . . Well, Ken Pope, see, his thing was like why rely on Max Tron to short a circuit or whatever when you could just as easily arrange an official blackout or whatever. Well you can imagine Ken Pope at city hall, I mean he was like in and out of doors and cubicles from one bureaucrat to another, he was everywhere, he didit all. But then what happened, all of that tubed the moment Ken Pope noticed Albert wearing this friendship bracelet given to him by some chicken number Ken Pope had given the bracelet to. Well Ken Pope fa-reaked!

—Liz Klutch

It was not like there was any promotion of some happening scene in the foredawn hour of the moon. Calls went out by word of mouth and telepathy. People came from their shadows.

Minutes come max would not find the square overflowing, nor was this midnight of anybody's soul.

Weird to imagine slaves bought and sold here.

That was Canal Street that slavetrading happened. This was where folks got hung.

Center of the city, right here.

Fiddler Ron was high on the scene: "Man, half the Quarter nightshift is out here!"

The Beadlady sat against a littercan making scatterchatter (weird to the uninitiated, otherwise duly shined on). Suddenstop cut to quiet even woke a drunk. It was then that the lights went out on the square. Instant native repose took effect. The clock up the belltower, stuck on moontime, spoofed on time gone the way of the lights.

No booze, no food, no music even, still people came, and stayed.

Matt Dockery and his cameracarrying live ones were still on their feet after closing Bourbon Street. Dockery had persuaded them was travelers not tourists would make a scene like this.

"In case you don't remember us from midnight, you were rude to my wife then, and if you don't apologize for that, I'm going to be angry at you for a long time, and I don't like to be that way, but if you don't apologize for being rude to my wife, I'm going to be angry at you for a long time."

Hidden Dave Crossway remembered from midnight; same as then he led with his eyes: "I apologize for being rude."

Longdeep sigh: "Thank you." Handshake shook—"Thank you."

Dockery all over the coverage: "Good man!"

The woman strictly *wha?*

Local play got stood in good humor. Not like he managed any smiles for the camera, but he did turn his best side.

Afterthought *who woulda thunk it?*

Gates open all sides of the common posed a throwback to wino jungle times. (Folks coming naked Albert Johnson dubbed "innocents abroad.") Absent the establishment artist scene, the square took on underdog overtones, strictly nonhustle.

At a fencefront hung with portraits and landscapes (in varying stages of progress, not to say neglect), Paul Arness was the lone holdover (albeit hardly representative) of the regular daytime artist scene. (Notwithstanding his dark apparel offsetting fuzzy moonshot graytowhite hair would recall his onetime latenight television ghosthost role vamping commercial breaks on *Creature Feature.*) Some biker and his old lady sitting for a portrait while Paul regaled onlookers with Shakespeare and Hollywood left one observer shaking his head: "Bikers in pastels and he doesn't get his feelings hurt! Who else but Paul?" Turns out here was one crowdpleaser would bolt on bikers quick as any other sitting subjects. Paul went Byzantine with a borrowed scarf for headwrap, profiling for the people: "In the words of Dean Martin: 'That's a Moor, eh?' Then he declaimed the lament of the lover who had *"loved not wisely, but too well."* Actually brought himself to tears falling on Desdemona to die on a kiss. The people loved it. In Othello's afterglow Paul recalled being discovered on this very plaza for a cameo in *Easy Rider* (what else but the acid trip sequence in St. Louis Cemetery?), and what was more, his beautiful friend Peter Fonda insisted to this day there must be a leading role for him in some major production. Most of these people knew Paul and his scene and could tell you no artist on the square pulled less easeltime. Even the biker and his old lady had heard the *Easy Rider* pitch. Still people paused and caught the act, and the plaza rang their rounds of applause. And the biker and his old lady—left sitting— kept sitting. Paul was Paul was Paul was all.

At The Gabildo, Buddy Talutta, Maitre D' upto Dugan's Beanwagon, otherwise known as Miss Buddy, presented an installation entitled "Modern Mythology." It featured Miss Buddy in quasidrag, seated on oak grain retouched red enamel, attended by dolls Barbie and Ken in matching sets. It was tableau of the androgynous deity Hype (Miss Buddy in mock polyester worthy of The Beadlady) presiding over generic personae (Barbie and Ken portraying—not to say parodying—themselves). Monotheon would be Miss Buddy's coinage for the divine order of Hype and Hype only. A posted sidebar read: *"Remember the good old days when we had real plastic."*

A little bit of powder, a little bit of paint, makes Miss Buddy look what she ain't. If tonight was a long one, last night was longer—guest of the DA on charges of doings done at The House of Abandon. Turns out the already notorious people's exhibit still standing formed the centerpiece of prosecution evidence for The People vs Joseph "Buddy" Talutta.

Proffit had his truck, Joe Bananas his.

Proffit's intention to unload his outrider was a job for Forbert and Doc. Soon as Joe Bananas heard Proffit calling Leo, he got on the air, remind him Leo's radio was busted.

Absent the sweeper machine, it was left Leo and the boys to jam gutterbottoms to truckbed with piles Hidden Dave had left up and down Bourbon Street. Leo wised up the boys on the Q.T. what Saturday nights the Sweeper was down, likely Brother Burke (the Sweeper driver) was overto The Gloworm overto Algiers—and what was more than coincidence about that was lining Proffit's pockets (Leo had seen cash pass hands at The Hummingbird). Forbert and Doc just kept crossing looks.

Talk was curtailed by Ruthie the Ducklady carried out Lafitte's knocked out loaded. Nothing new here (recently Doc and Hidden Dave had carried Ruthie home from Pete's Bistro across the street). They fetched Ruthie (and her boombox) some truckseat next Leo; Forbert rode shotgun and Doc driverside runningboard round Ruthie's place down Chartres Street. Leo waited while they got her inside. There could be no cutting away quick enough from her odor of stale beer to the pore. But Ruthie rallied to head off the break, calling from her room howbout turning on the air conditioner. Then she wanted water. Scooping duckdrop proved the final concession of municipal time. (Not unlike her timely revival the time with Hidden Dave: one after another rearguard project sprung between the good guys and the door.) Doc had to say these ducklady rescues were looking more ducklady than rescue. What they came back to out on the street was Leo gone and Proffit and Joe Bananas waiting.

Upto the Moonwalk, crest of the levee, forefield St. Louis Cathedral and Jackson Square, they laid the man in peestained floodlength candystripe pants on a bench looking out at the Mississippi River.

He woke not knowing where he was or how he got there, nevermind was he woke for true and howcome was that. Sooner or later he knew what he knew: *Moonspooked waters along moonspooked Algiers far bank*; thought within a thought *one River assbackwards* even heard his voice say it: like he saw it and could swear to it till he said so and it shifted . . .

Figure upwalkway, moving on down: Crossblooded woman, fitted for notice: low cut, high hemmed—seethru anyhow. Cottonmouth moccasins either shoulder: impression *got more snake on'er than clothes* Mug *hubbahubba*

"Wouldja believe it? Them waters run backward, by God, I seen it myself I did."

"Who's that chosen to witness the truth?"

". . . Huh?"

"The waters turned when the moon did."

"*Hot damn!*"

Leo Dazzolini was running a dumpload out to Lafitte Street Incinerator, upto Rampart Street he noticed Tex Rowe and

Flat Annie Pratt hung on each other like the wild man and wilder woman responsible for Tommy Blaha. Tex heard Leo coming, him and Flat Annie flagged Sanitation transportation down Jackson Square. However uneremonious their arrival by garbagetruck, the more so was meeting Proffit on the scene.

Proffit shook his head, "Ahm not even gonna ask."

Tex said, "You don't wanna know."

Flat Annie said, "This already happened!"

Proffit and Tex crossed looks.

Flat Annie said, "I could swear it was like we were all here before, and you said you weren't gonna ask."

Proffit said, "Somebody on this corner is headed rounna bend, ah can see dat right now."

Tex stagewhispered, "Gets ahead of herself sometimes."

Proffit shrugged, "Shizza fast woman."

Flat Annie kept saying, "I could swear it was just like it already happened."

Tex said, "Look back on somp'n ain't even done happenin yet it's a mind movin too fast, wouldn' y'say?"

Proffit said, "Sounna me like somebody been grubbin sommadat hippiecake gittin passed aroun heh tonight."

Flat Annie said, "When wuzza last time either a you seen a shootin star?"

Proffit said, "Did ah say headed rounna bend? Make dat gone."

Tex said, "Howzat for somp'n already happened?"

Flat Annie told Tex, "Tell me you don't love it!"

Tex told Flat Annie, "Not my mother's son."

They kissed thru smirks.

Leo Dazzolini, hung back with his mouth open, checked in raised up with his hand: "Ahm gonna Lafitte 'treet, y'all—umma go 'n' keep on gone what umma do!" Tagged it a gutbucketbust of a laugh.

Big Jim Bullshit bought a luckybead off The Beadlady, told her hold the change for a twentydollarbill. The Beadlady hung it mug *I can do that* otherwise said, "Who you see holdin no change? Don't no twentyspot make a token foddat luckybead, don't talk to me how you mekkin me no lagniappe." Big Jim Bullshit ask, "What I'm scorin for luck here anyhow?" The Beadlady answered, "Now no time soon you won't see no jailtime." Due fanfare was Big Jim Bullshit put a kiss on his new luckybead bought and prayed for even money.

Down the grass, inside the gates, Bev bellydown for backrub, Liz laying on hands—talking Bobo:

"He was on us every dumpstop till George and Doc lost their cart."

"That figures. I mean you gotta know any chance of you coming up short would be must see entertainment for Bobo, dear."

"Anyway, now you know why the change of heart about me on the truck."

"I might've expected his insinuating smirk insinuated something I wasn't gonna care for."

Herecome Fiddler Ron: "Hey dudes. What's a buzz?"

Milo said, "Could be the proverbial time outta mind, not dark of night, not daylight either."

Hidden Dave said, "Ever seen moonshadow leave a trace?"

United Cab Ronnie said, "Well, y'know, you talk about afteraffect, it's like this observation I once read about things lit by hurricane lamps somehow making exceptionally vivid memory traces. Howcome that would be I dunno, but the point is I could see that sorta carryover coming outta this light. I mean how all this shakes out in memory could prove interesting."

Earshot, other conversation, Albert Johnson (in all his visionary stature due originator of such a down scene) was giving his take: "Needless to say, I'm pleased to see the cathedral looking less like a stageprop, but my favorite impression, if you care to know, is that banksoftheNile effect of the spiked palms, which is exquisite."

Milo tranced off: "Somethin what OoooseBadoose says about the morning star reflecting waking life reeling back to Divine Memory. His thing about human consciousness turning the feedback loop of creation."

Hidden Dave said, "His Lord of Eden characterization was what got me. The 'glorified bagman shipping karma' line."

Meantime, OoooseBadoose got a figment on   *(midsquare)* *a great live oak preplace of the Colonel Jackson statue*   subspect *Tree of Life tableau Adam and Eve coupled in Serpent surround underglow of cherubs up with a flaming sword* (his ensemble icon for Divine Memory).

Herecome Luman Harris (tourbuggydriver got the byword howcome the French Market never closed), side by side his old mule Hutch; man and mule styling lids of Goldberg's, Luman a straw mock stetson with a peacock plume, Hutch a sombrero with customfitted earpokes; serenade to hoofbeats: "*A Shining Path I Walk With Thee.*"

"What it is, muleskinnerman?"

"Hardtime rollover action out they."

"For true?"

"Rollover action ta burn."

"Go head."

"Slowridin home all we wuz, so hep me. Ain' fret no getalong no tired mule ain' got, knowt ahm sayin, jez moseyin along, nice 'n' easylike. Well donchu know we jam us a pothole, ah mean it dump us a *hurtin*. Frontside slam down, backside liff up, ass over tincup we go. Pothole damnside flip us like a flapjack. Man come side say, 'Gawd give us a pothole 'n' thas way He put it.' Umma tella man, say, Yeah you right, say, Farside *His* pothole they a hitch leff fa broke, hyeh me 'n' ole Hutch, praise the Lawd, bless ah souls, we count ah blessins, hiz'n my'ns, we up'n walkin, ain' ah asses bustes."

Somebody said, "Potholes down these streets wannabe craters on the moon."

Luman say, "You know it too?"

United Cab Ronnie said, "City fathers probably sooner pitch singlelane moontop for tourist promotion than fill any potholes for the people."

"Ahm tellinya."

Joe Bananas said, "Pavements in the Quarters ain't noways but down you don't watch out."

"You ain' neva lie."

Hidden Dave Crossway cut acrossplaza to a pushcart stowed in an alcove, then back his tracks, shovel in hand, put a move on muledrop down on the common. Luman went overtheshoulder motioning thanks—he was looking out at the scene, talking what it is: "Someplace all moon like dis hyeh make a spell on people's minds, knowt ahm sayin? Ain' nuttin shakin no konna way, but shonuff somp'n goin on hyeh, awyeah. Place all moon like dis hyeh? Lawd have mercy . . ."

Meantime Hutch scored freerange feed on grass waybackwhen cushion of many a wino stupor. His withers shuddered to the touch of a barebreasted woman.

Witnesses up Moonwalkway swore some ship passing downriver doffed lights. Others insisted it never happened, that the ship sailed upriver not down and anyway without ceremony. Some said there was no ship.

Moonspect of the square took on new dimension as the woman with the snakes appeared with the man in the peestained floodlength candystripe pants. In her aspect this woman waxed measure of the moment sway to pool a gallery or part one. The man just tagged along—way long—as in snakelong, waywide alongside. Without notice he might shake his head/say to himself, "I'm got religion or gone bughouse, one." (By now just being on his feet tricked odds, and what was more, he was not hungover. He would not recall a cocobutt tripping a door alarm, nor any asswhuppin between him and his last five bucks, and far as any river caught assbackwards turn of moontide, chances were he forgot that too.)

"Ahright, PeeCandy!"

"Got a cigarette you could spare, brother?"

"Don't smoke, me."

"Neither do I, but I'm tryin like hell."

Northwest corner of the square, root of a golden raintree, OoooseBadoose was down on deep sitting; subspect *daybreak east over the west bank* active principle:

Sheer geologic sleight of land misdirection turn of the riverbend

The woman with the snakes found OoooseBadoose in his silence. He was no sooner open with his eyes upto her, he made with the hallmark pitch for small change, his abrupt "Ooosebadoose!" by way of howdydoo. Somebody said, "What he said?" She came across sweeter than the price of beans and rice: she offered him a peach. OoooseBadoose went slack in the mug. They crossed teeming looks his upnod thanks to her trace smile.

Milo took benchtop offside somebody familiar.

"Man at Takee Outee took a slug thru the lovehandle. Probably be discharged by noon."

Eyes met across moonspect.

"The streetsweep."

"The one used as a shield."

Lookaway gaze: "Muthafucka tolme grab ma own damn salt."

"That explains that."

Penitentiary face on: "So what it is you mean to do with what it is you know?"

Milo sparked a bone and offered it: "One hit sacrament cool?"

Stone penitentiary still: "Streetsweep keep cool sweep again, knowt ahm sayin?"

"Health alert well taken."

"Bad side of me a man see only once."

"I pass a mean salt shaker."

"We cool way we at now, bra?"

"I'm cool if you're cool."

"Ahright, ma man."

Stone penitentiary to outbreath afterglow:

"Glad the man gonna be ahright."

"Glad you're glad."

"Ahright."

Brothers in headship down on moonspect.

Daytime Johnny Omen and Jivin Jeff Dean made the scene after Jivin Jeff's gig with The Babaloo Indians overto La Casa. Daytime Johnny had passed by La Casa flush from his sabbath at Moondip Minnie's opening for Bootlip Russell and the impromptu finale with Sweet Emma Barrow.

Foredawn Decatur Street was practically a mall between the Moonwalk and Jackson Square. Daytime Johnny was blown away: "Stone fuckin beautiful, man! All these people all night down with the moon! I mean how cool izzat?"

Inside the gates, midcommon, people kept hushed tones.

Mary Mosely said, "Funny you should appear. We're talking about Alvin Lee. Either of you heard from him?"

Jivin Jeff nodded, "Alvin's bustin the chitlin circuit with Dirty Doug and the Backdoor Men."

Shushubaby said, "Sounds Alvin's speed."

Mary Mosley asked, "Dirty Doug and the Backdoor Men! Since when?"

Jivin Jeff said, "Check this out. Week ago maybe your friend 'n' mine collect from Biloxi, right? Could I send money?"

Shushubaby said, "Sounds like Alvin all right."

Jivin Jeff said, "Well then he calls from Mobile: He's got this gig, right? Cancel the cash. Thing was I had already sent some. Noon next day the money comes back from Panama City."

Shushubaby said, "You got money back from Alvin?"

Jivin Jeff said, "How's that for being on the level about a gig?"

Mary Mosley said, "Lemme ask you. Does the name Pamela Hardesty mean anything to you?"

Jivin Jeff said, "I know who Pamela Hardesty is, yeah," and Daytime Johnny said, "Assets into the next room," and Jivin Jeff said, "Feet don't get wet in the shower."

Mary Mosley told them, "That'll be fine."

Matt Dockery spoke up: "Not to mention she's married to a city official practiced in toxicology of sorts."

Daytime Johnny said, "Could be thereby hangs a tale I heard at The Dip."

Mary Mosley said, "Same story I heard same place, I wonder?"

Daytime Johnny like to broke it down stoptime: "Stickman hits on a Garden District squeeze; Dr. No performs corrective surgery; Stickman wakes up dickless in Arabi; faithless lady gets the missing part Special D."

Mary Mosley been nodding all along: "Same sordid story."

Brooklyn Bob said, "Talk about a sting, man. That's a sting."

Jivin Jeff knowing different all the way: "It's a whodonit what ain't nobody done nothin, man. Here's the thing. What Alvin told me, the way it went down, somebody sent Pamela Hardesty one of those mail order chocolateflavor candycocks, y'know, like the ones you see listed in alternative classifieds?"

Brooklyn Bob said, "A statement is made!"

Matt Dockery commented, "That in itself is weird enough."

Jivin Jeff said, "Open to question who it was sent the cock."

United Cab Ronnie shrugged, "Insinuating husband."

Jivin Jeff nodded, "Logical suspect."

Brooklyn Bob said, "Racially charged as a chocolate flavor candycock? Me, I suspect it was Newberry sent the cock."

Mary Mosley told him, "You're one to talk, Bob. For all we know it was you sent the cock," and Shushubaby said,

"Yeah, man. Leave Newberry alone," and Mary Mosley told Shushubaby, "Thank you."

United Cab Ronnie said, "Anybody else pickin up on a mail order caper gone south in a rumor mill?"

Jivin Jeff said, "Make that deep south," and Mary Mosley said, "Really."

Daytime Johnny said, "What we have here is a bucket brigade between the inside story and the story on the street."

Shushubaby said, "Alvin says black people are crazy but white people are sick."

Dockery commented, "Some inspired pillowtalk called down there."

Hidden Dave Crossway went retro: "Classmate of mine at Columbia, Southern boy outta Roanoke name of Billy Makepiece, once found this *Village Voice* listing for fruitflavor candycocks and sent one to the university president. Turns out during the student takeover of the administration building that year a fruitflavor cock was found in a safe."

Miss Buddy Talutta, at a stop on a stroll, said, "People's Exhibit for The Establishment vs The Revolution."

Brooklyn Bob smirked, "Merits of the case too familiar for comfort, Miss Buddy?"

Miss Buddy answered at a fadeaway sashay: "Excuse me while I go take a douche."

Voice called out: "Viva La House of Abandon Revue!"

Dockery said, "Anybody consider maybe Alvin Lee sent the mucho macho himself?"

Mary Mosley said, "Talk about stirring things up."

Dockery said, "Exactly. An inside joke got dirty outside."

United Cab Ronnie spoke up: "All I gotta say is there's a whole lotta spin from a mail order cock to a trophy in a specimen jar. Some storytellers out there gotta be plenty over their heads reconciling that weave."

Mary Mosley said, "I've been all night long keeping what I heard in confidence, but most people I talked to already knew."

Brooklyn Bob said, "As if getting gossip without giving gossip does not a busybody make."

Mary Mosley hairyeyeballed Brooklyn Bob for that.

Shushubaby said, "Oh well. Everything works out for the best if you let it."

Jivin Jeff said, "Man, I'll tellya what, since Alvin crashed at my place, I dunno how many times I've been all hours of the night chasin away floozies leanin on my doorbell lookin for Alvin Lee."

Shushubaby said, "Like Alvin says, the wide on for him don't quit by itself."

Dockery said, "Do I hear right that you would attest to that?"

Shushubaby was innocence in the heartround—blushing like a schoolgirl but not back a beat: "You heard right."

Hidden Dave spoke up, "Who's a thinking stiff's cure?"

Streetcrew romance in the GreatAllBecoming.

Suspect a thingstiff's cure.

Congratulations in a roundabout way. You made me come.

How'd that happen?

I dunno.

I predict someday somebody'll bring your butter like Alvin Lee did.

I wish you could.

Sorry I didn't assay like I could have that time.

I'm being a bitch, I know.

Hey, you're a throwback to simpler times.

Yeah, right.

No, really. Your man brings home the meat or he can go run with the hunt. I like your style.

You're a sweet talkin man, that's for sure.

However true to form any orgy I'm at is liable to be a circle jerk.

Brother called himself Junior. Penitentiaryface to brother in headship this was a changed man. Still down on moonspect him and Milo; they were signifying and then some.

Local dowager comes wanting could she sit: aftermath a cockroach situation, she was all spread out: "Well seeing that thing tangled in that poor girl's hair was hard to look at, let me tell you. And that *god*awful crunch underfoot, oh, the *thought* makes me *cringe*! As if this city crawling with those awful things isn't caution enough, well do you know those buggers can fly to boot! Mind you, when my Aunt Kaka was alive—well, she's not dead yet but she's in the hospital (*yuks out Junior and Milo*). . . Anyway, you probably don't need to be hearing all this."

Junior said, "M'am, them cockroaches could take over this city anytime they want to, you mean you ain' realizzat?"

Woman said, "Now that is what I would call a revolting development!"

Milo said, "Righteous thing cockroaches aren't greedy as some people."

Junior said, "You waitsee ain' cockroaches still hyeh affa peoples all gone."

Woman said, "Lord in Heaven have mercy on the faithful."

Woman name of Pauline DeSilva, lived at the Pontalba, balcony commanding the square. Middle of the night she woke in strange light, balcony view not typical of the hour: people leaning into hushed conversation . . . cathedral chimes forward of the hour on the clock   Citytime she got down there in a taffeta robe. In her agitation lights out on the square passed notice by pale of the moon

Pauline said, "You know, it's the strangest thing. From my balcony there where I live I could've sworn I saw a face I haven't seen since we both saw something neither of us was ready for and people can't believe or don't want to anyway."

Milo quoted: "*Face of faces from bygone times longer by than gone.*"

Pauline said, "For what it's worth, this is not something I talk about, but you seem sensitive, so I suppose I can tell you. Years ago (you'll recognize when) I went to Ft. Worth for a wedding. Well that Friday we went into Dallas, these artist friends and me; we thought we might do some errands and maybe get in a little shopping before the rehearsal that evening. Well around noon we were enjoying a picnic on some grass just outside of the business district there, when along comes this man with a camera, you know, well he was all in a dither about a presidential motorcade about due to pass. Mind you, we weren't political people, particularly, I mean the President's visit was all over town, of course, but little did we know this motorcade would be actually passing our way; here, come to find out, we had stumbled onto this roadside view, of all things. Well at some point I happened to glance up this sort of a slope behind us there, and I noticed this man under a tree in back of this wall at the top of the hill there, you know, he was up there in the shade looking over the wall. I didn't think much of it at the time, particularly, just somebody watching for the President, same as we were. So along comes this motorcade with all of this fanfare, you know, what with all of these official cars and this noisy motorcycle escort and what have you. Well let me tell you, the President and First Lady were something to see, all smiling and waving in that noonday sun. Mind you, I was so taken, silly me, I guess I sent one of them a kiss. Not to suggest that the President ever even noticed, really, although I like to think that he did, at least he smiled and waved in my direction, whether or not at me directly, Lord only knows, anyway, then I remember he was turning, sort of facing away at someone else in the car or something, next thing I know he was seizing at himself, I mean he snapped like a martinet, it was like this seizure was happening, you know, his hands went up to his throat (like this), you see, and his elbows all winged out wide, and he got this long gone kind of a look about him, I'll never forget it, this long gone kind of a look in his eyes. And right then, that very instant, on some unknown impulse, I don't know why, you know how you get these impulses out of nowhere sometimes, well for some reason I glanced up that hill again, and right when I did, that man I had noticed up there, I couldn't believe it, well do you know he had this gun and he was shooting it. The instant I looked there he was aiming thru this scope thing and the gun going off that very instant, right when I looked. That would be when my artist friends, they were still looking on when I looked away, see, they even saw the President's head shatter. That was just how they described it, that dear head just shattered all over the backseat of that limosine, they said. Well as you might expect, what those people saw in plain view that afternoon has haunted them ever since, bless their souls. But anyway, what I remember next was the President's foot, that was all you could see, just the sole of his shoe poking out that backseat windowside; and the First Lady with blood all over her clothes, you know; and the man on the hill dropping from view up there behind the wall; and the man with the camera running for his life. And I'll never forget all those official cars and motorcycles all speeding away under this overpass, and some of the people up there on the overpass, they were pointing to the hilltop behind where we were, you know. Well I mean to tell you, it was something. People dashing every which way, you know, people down on the ground for cover. I'll never forget this man and a woman on the ground shielding these two little children. Oh, it was something all right."

Milo said, "That's alotta story to carry."

Pauline DeSilva said, "I feel like I can talk to you."

Junior told her, "Me 'n' ma man here we know what it is to see more'n what it is you come lookin for."

Pauline said, "You know, to this day it amazes me how anyone could be so utterly unperturbed at a time like that. Here this man had just shot the President for petesake. Well you would've thought it was all in a day's work. The assassination was over, time to leave so he was leaving. No rush, no worry; just pack up and go. Calm and collected as he could be. Can you imagine? The unmitigated gall of some people!"

Milo said, "Have gun, will travel,"

Junior said, "Wear it out, ma man."

Pauline said, "Afterward there were all of these people showing badges, you know, these detective type men in plainclothes showing these badges. Well this man comes rushing from that overpass that I mentioned—same man I could swear I just saw, by the way, as if he would recognize me after all of these years, improper as I am in these nightslippers and robe out in public—well anyway, he's scrambling all around, you know, this man from the overpass, I mean to tell you he was positively beside himself, pointing up that hill there, insisting no end he had seen a man shoot the President. Well, no surprise, I suppose, any supporting eyewitness information I could lend should only meet what his met. Why you would've thought we were a couple of crackpots or something. Can you imagine? They did not so much as look where we told them we had seen this man with a gun."

Junior said, "Sound like stealer's choice was they in on the chase or in on the getaway."

"Well let me tell you. When I reported what I saw to the local authorities, I told them, I said, I don't know about this man that you're holding, but I can tell you the man that I saw wasn't him. And what's more, I told them, I said, So help me God, same as I turned exactly when I turned and looked exactly which way I looked, I believe sure as anything the shot I saw fired was the one that killed the President. Well they thanked me for the information and that was the end of the information. Now I ask you, what kind of a way was that?"

Milo said, "Your rendezvous with destiny got censored outta history. You get to keep the unauthorized assassination."

"Well you would think that it would rub people to their very souls to imagine that someone could simply up and get away with such a thing."

Milo said, "A prospect not lost on the sponsors of the official assassination, I suspect."

Pauline said, "Maybe I'm some kind of fool, I dunno, but a part of me still believes that the people deserve to know the truth."

Junior said, "Somebody got they story 'n' they stickin to it."

Milo said, "Lemme ask you something. Any chance

you'd recall a man opening an umbrella? I realize that might sound a bit offthewall, but there's speculation this man might've been operating in some sorta maestro of the shoot type capacity, so to speak. I'm just wondering if maybe you might've had something on that. It's available in photo archives, by the way."

Pauline said, "Well of all the rarefied notions! The very suggestion of an accomplice that near at hand gives me the creeps even now, if you really wanna know. What I do remember and won't forget ever is that man shooting the gun."

Milo asked, "Somebody you could describe or identify, this man with the gun?"

Pauline said, "A glimpse I caught of him dropping from view behind that wall up there was about the only halfway decent look I had of him."

Milo nodded, "Executioner's face was well hidden. Probably the best targetline on the motorcade route. Man was a pro."

Pauline said, "Then again, you know how some things somehow you just know sometimes?"

Milo said, "You were there when these times we live in hit overdrive. A thing like that would make an impression. Somehow you'd know again sameway you knew waybackwhen."

Pauline said, "I'll tell you what gets me, though, what with all of these probes and investigations and what have you thru the years, it's all these mysterious deaths and disappearances they've had. Witnesses found dead, witnesses lost without a trace. Why it's enough to give me pause about calling attention to myself."

Junior said, "Did that man know about you like you know about him, you'd know by now, don't you worry."

Milo said, "Anyway, it's not like the leader of the free world blown away right in front of you has to be the defining moment of your life, y'know. Far as that goes, it may be about you seeing things other people don't see."

Pauline said, "You know, to this day there's a part of me that still can't believe that ever really happened. In my mind I keep seeing that car speed away in that noonday sun."

Junior said, "Listen ahm sayin. Last thing the man ever see in this world some fine lady send him a kiss, well dig, you gotta know he give it up callin'at good, knowt ahm sayin?"

Pauline DeSilva said, "Pray tell, wear it out, I'm sure," and they all laughed.

Laughs *headship of headships* laughs.

Matt Dockery buttonholed Hidden Dave Crossway foot of the Colonel Jackson statue: "That was a fine thing you did over there before."

Hidden Dave shrugged it off, "Good people."

Dockery said, "I couldn't believe it. Not only does away with countertourist cynicism—he apologizes even!"

Hidden Dave said, "Must be the moon."

Dockery said, "Must be. Man, I still don't believe it."

Hidden Dave said, "They promised to send proof if the pictures turn out."

Milo recognized Art Nieman on the scene:

"Still standing, I see."

"Yeah, well, hey, for all the drug 'n' alcohol abuse I could fit into one night, this is what a zombie looks like."

"There's a survivor."

"Right now it's looking like my parkingplace could be the next frontier."

"You wanna be legal. These towtruck turks enjoy their work."

"Burned down house for sale is my landmark."

"*No Parking At No Time* painted on the sidewalk?"

"You know the place!"

"You're at Maison Bananas . . ."

Joe Bananas putting this story to the touch upto Barranco's (supposedly on the Q.T. to Big Jim Bullshit—not to mention anybody and everybody prone to be buttonholed): "Yeah, ahm bringin down some goon action outta Chicago. Buddy o' mine gotta tuyn some jack pretty quick. Ah tol'im ahd make a few phonecalls."

Turns out the homegrown (Ninth Ward) talent had it going on about like Joe Bananas had contacts in Chicago:

"Don't talk to me no bullshit whichway no wind wuz at, son, ahm tellinya, y'set da wrong fuckin house on fiye, you fuckin iwwitowits . . ."

Nieman got talking with George Forbert:

"My best guess would be you were a navy man."

"Negative."

"The Section 8 he mentioned."

"Never happened."

"Not to pry, man, I'm just sayin, Section 8 is a discharge not a deferment, see, that's howcome I'm makin with the military bit, know what I'm sayin?"

"What happened was my sophomore year in college I got busted while I was tripping on acid and wound up in a mental institution instead of jail."

"Guess that locked up your deferment status."

"Not really. I got outta the hospital and back in school."

"Major in sanitary engineering? I presume."

"Close."

"Just joshin ya, man."

"Actually my major was psychology."

"Man, some heavy minds I'm seein pushin brooms around here, I'm tellinya."

"Sanctuary of lapsed scholars."

"Lapsed scholars, uh?"

"Guy over here, Johnny Albesharpe, stalled a termpaper short his final three credits for an anthropology degree."

"Termpaper he never wrote about says it all for the market value of that degree."

"Guy with the shades, Hidden Dave, got kicked outta Columbia for antiwar activities."

"Right on."

"You know Milo—"

"Major dude."

"Springbreak roadtrip outta Rutgers—he never looked back."

"Ahright. Transfer Road Scholar. I love it!"

"Shushubaby—"

"Shu *who* baby?"

"Hippie name. Anyway, she flunked outta Maryland."

"Ummm hmmm. And howbout this other dude I saw pushin a broom?"

"Albert Johnson, yeah, Albert's no refugee, Albert's an omniversity bon vivant."

"Omniversity, uh? Howbout you? You omniversity?"

"Strictly conventional one dimensional. Undergrad thing at Boston U."

"Sheepskin?"

"For what it's worth."

"Man, it's an up 'n' walkin alternative unit you lapsed scholars're puttin on the street, I must say."

After Buford making the scene with war stories from The Funk Shop could only be Liz holding court: "Nobody but nobody is eightysixed more places, including some places nobody else is, and even some places nobody else ever was."

Beverly Griffin said, "Including The Funk Shop."

Liz said, "Exactly. I mean him even being in there is what I don't get."

. . . passing glimpse Buford cut by The Funk Shop was Louise Broussard up top the bar at her gutbucket edge wailing "These Old Brown Shoes Keep Walking Back To You." Buford heard that, he threw down with The Funk Shop experience:

. . . Dickinthedirt acted on faith in due slack by reason he was drunk. Couple bros walked in with a different set of assumptions. Dickinthedirt came off with some bluegum nigger jive would they open wide could he looksee inside—he was still on the floor when Buford left the building . . .

Buford said, "Actually he was catching the bum's rush at the time."

Bev said, "It's called Duke City limits on the Dickinthedirt express."

Liz said, "What's that Bootlip Russell line? '*Womb to tomb mouth first.*'"

Milo spoke up: "*Epitaph Blues.*"

Shushubaby said, "Like that time Johnny came outta Lu and Charlie's drunk and these dudes hit'im up for money and Johnny told'em to suck shit thru a rag. Well they just beat the shit outta him."

Bev said, "Was that the time he woke up with some old man bent over him asking was this the bus stop?"

Shushubaby said, "That was the time."

Big Jim Bullshit said, "Hey, well you heard about Dirty Ernie passed out on somebody's doorstep up here on Dumaine Street. Morningtime some man leavin out the house tripped over'im. Nothin but cool about it, though. Even brung Dirty Ernie coffee. Dirty Ernie said all that done was git'm a wide awake drunk."

Shushubaby eyed Milo: "Tell about the time you left that party on Mandeville Street."

Milo said, "Leaving the party was about the last thing I remember."

Art Nieman said, "Uh oh. Many's a setback begins with leaving a party."

Milo said, "Not a bad setback for selective memory either."

Shushubaby said, "I'll refresh your memory. What happened was Milo left this party on Mandeville Street and passed out in the backseat of some strange car. Well whenever these two lovers showed up, they musta really been wrapped up in each other, they drove all the way uptown and never even realized he was back there. Well anyway, so when he woke up . . . you go ahead and tell it."

Milo said, "Well, y'see, it was like this. I figured I'd rally for a comeback at the party, but then I wiped out over this picket fence I coulda swore wasn't there last I passed. Trouble was the neighborhood crimewatch took an interest before I caught on to the change of address. I was more or less gettin my shit together when these voices behind flashlights brought the news."

Shushubaby said, "Lucky for you the cops were nice and gave you a lift home."

Milo said, "Service above and beyond, this is true."

Art Nieman said, "Man, what is it with this guy? He

draws the heat, he gets a lift home. Heat's on me, man—eyecontact call: Guest of the DA every time."

Big Jim Bullshit said, "Man, you wanna talk eyecontact call, check this out, man, any probation personnel you got goes off anything like the leather number I got, you're lookin out they don't reopen Alcatraz for you, man, then is when eyecontact call is eyecontact call, you hear like I'm sayin atcha?"

Nieman said, "Hey, I'm hearin ya, man. Feature this shit. Selective Service waiting room, right? Wall to wall talent. Bulldog sergeant looks in: 'I need three volunteers for the Corps—you, you and you!' I'm goin, Fuck me dead, man. My ticket to Nam done just been writ."

Hidden Dave said, "I've heard tell of that recruiting device, although the guy I heard it from was never even in the military. Sort of assumed this incountry cowboy identity scooped off Nam vets at group therapy or something."

Liz said, "Are you serious? Now whatever on earth would possess somebody to pose as a Vietnam veteran, for heavensake?"

Hidden Dave shrugged: "Roleplayin buzz. Kinduva secondhand self concept sorta thing. You bypass the experience and run fast and loose with somebody else's story. Some time or other we all do it, more or less."

Liz said, "I beg your pardon."

Milo said, "Self concept makeover old as dirt. Actually I could see personal story revision having tonic applications. Kinduva lucid memory type thing. You revise memory sameway lucid dreamers revise dreams. It's applied phoniness with real possibilities."

Albert Johnson fingerpointed Milo: "Seize that man, he's a fool!"

• • •

Nieman buttonholed Hidden Dave first chance. "Lemme ask y'somp'n, man. I gotta know. The dude with the secondhand self concept you mentioned. Wuzzat on the level?"

Hidden Dave said, "Actually that was a variation on an old hitchhiking device. You smile and wave at the person driving by. Sooner or later, I guarantee ya, somebody pulls over wonderin where you know each other from. Whenever I'd apologize for the deception, people would say, no, hey, it gotcha the ride. Even made some new friends."

Nieman was onto Hidden Dave doing Hidden Dave like Hidden Dave was onto Nieman doing Nieman: "I'm hip, man. Here's the thing. That secondhand self concept truth attack you put down; man, that found me in a crowd, I mean that went right by everybody right to where my head is at. Man, I knew right then and there I'd logged my last klick in country."

Hidden Dave soulfisted: "Truth over self limitation."

Nieman said, "Takes a load off, man."

Hidden Dave said, "City of masks we're onto here. Stories get taken on, stories get taken off. You can do that here."

Nieman said, "The others went AWOL on the uptake, man. They took the misdirection."

Hidden Dave said, "Some things are between two people."

Nieman nodded, "So it was intentional."

Hidden Dave said, "Honorable discharge."

Nieman said, "Fuckin street crew, man, I swear."

Hidden Dave said, "Within country mission accomplished."

Nieman guffed off: "Hey, we a couple within country cowboys or what?"

Prebrother handshake a thing within a thing between two people.

Nieman came eye to eye with Buford Horseman otherside:

Buford said, "Are you gay?"

Nieman said, "No."

Buford said, "Nor am I."

Hidden Dave said, "Pure straight talk."

Nieman said: "Reminds me one time at a bar with my dad, some guy asked my dad was he gay, my dad hauled off and punched him in the face. I said, 'Dad, I don't believe it, you hit that guy.' Dad said, 'Some people you can talk to and some you hafta hit.'"

Buford said, "I would prefer not to incur fallout."

Nieman said, "No strain, man. I'm just sayin."

Buford said, "I did not intend to give offense."

Nieman said, "None taken. You just reminded me is all."

Buford said, "Just so you know, I'm prone to conniptions."

Nieman said, "Prone are ya?"

Buford said, "Anecdotal coldcocking insinuates applied coldcocking my conniption quotient goes straight up."

Hidden Dave said, "The old spastic trick. Nothin sidetracks an assbustin quite like convincing convulsions. I actually know of somebody faked out like that outright cut 'n' ran."

Junior (been eavesdropping) like to fell out: "Ma man he got somp'n for somebody bring him trouble. Don't be no asswhuppin don't no conniption come. He tickle me."

Nieman said, "I'm tellin ya, man. It's not like that. There's no hurt on here."

Hidden Dave said, "Coldcock advisory not in effect. Spastic alert inactive."

Buford said, "Roger that, if you will."

Contact crosscalls three people maybe four but anyhow not just two

Johnny Albesharpe showed up. He was hanging out with Beverly Griffin, Liz Klutch and Shushubaby. Next they knew was Joe Bananas breakin hushbustin bad.

". . . Well, the streets they clean, ah got no gripe widdat. It's like'is hyeh. Ah been all night out hyeh, ain't nobody ah seen push a broom, not a one all night. Anybody temme how them streets they clean ain't nobody ah seen push a broom all night? Don't gimme wrong now. Long azzem streets clean at's all ah care about. Ah'll tell you people same as ah tole ma people onna day crew. What ah tole ma day crew it's like'is hyeh. Long azzem streets clean we got no problem. Streets ain't clean, then *you* got a *big* problem. Simple azzat. Do ma thing, we got no problem; don't do ma thing, *you* got *big* problem. At's how ah operate. Umma teyya somp'n else, too, fuh y'alls infamation. Upto Lafitte Street it's pushcarts, see, they brand new, ain't neva been used: you see don't ah get dem out hyeh fa you people. Them damn crates you all pushin ain't no damn good fa nuttin. Ain' no kinda way ahm puttin no crew o' mine out no street wit no equipment like 'at it's brand new cawts upta Lafitte Street don't nobody use 'n' won't nobody miss, no kinda way in hell it ain't. Come Monday you waitsee don't ah have them cawts out hyeh fa you people. Little Joe lookin out fa ma crew. Remembadat."

Johnny said, "That's what I'd call steppin down with both feet."

By the grinding of Joe's dentures any fool could tell was plenty suckerpunch left in him for some wiseass making him out for no chump.

Bev said, "Joe, is it true what they say about you sucker-punched a seventy-five-year-old lady?"

Joe said, "Hon, ah could care less how old dat woman wuz. Anybody tuyn no hose on ma crew then on me gonna wear Little Joe upside the head, you get like ahm sayin? Say whatcha want about Little Joe, me ah stick up fa ma crew. Somebody mess wit ma crew, ah don't care who it is, no sense even lookin ova they shouldiz, ahm comin. Mess wit ma crew, dey mine, baby, dey mine. Damn sure one thing ain' no denyin. Don' nobody but nobody tuyns no hose on me—'n' ah do mean nobody, 'n' ah don' mean maybe."

Johnny said, "The way I heard it this seventy-five-year-old woman you suckerpunched didn't even go down."

"Who tolyadat?"

"It's in the report."

"You ain' seen no report, son. 'At's Directa's eyes only."

"Not his mouth only."

"Hey, you wanna know howcome 'at ole bag didn't go down? Umma teyya howcome she didn't go down. She didn't go down cuz she didn't know which end wuz up, at's howcome wuzzat. Wudn't all there to begin with, y'ast me."

Johnny said, "Word on the street was the old lady letcha punch yourself out."

"Git attayeh."

"Way I heard it she was takin over, you had all you could do just to hold on."

"One punch umma punch masef out? Get attayeh. You huyda down but not out? Well she wuz out but not down, you can ast anybody. Hey, ahm not proud ah clocked no hag, not none ahm not, but so hep me ain't nuttin umma take back neitha, umma teyyadat right nah. Don't make me no diffence it's a woman how old, ah could care less, me. Dat ole hag wearin Little Joe upside the head go to showya don't nobody mess wit ma crew. Somebody mess wit ma crew gonna pay huytn time. Mess wit ma crew dey gonna meet Little Joe. Remembadat."

Shiny new cadillac curbside Cabildo leave off Ramone. High heel echoes jump steady off cathedralface—stutterstep first blush a woman holding snakes; eyecontact call: "Muthafuck dat shit!" Turnabout, baby seen enough, baby make otherway: "Ain' no passway passway enough for me 'n' no fuckinmuthafuckin snake, baby, muthafuck dat shit . . ." Last seen makin St. Ann Street, direction Pete's and Lafitte's up Bourbon Street (status eightysixed both places subject to change depending who worked which door).

Oz jock Al Finkelstein down the grass with Poopdeck Perry of Baltimore:

Poopdeck told Finkelstein, "Golden grooveyard wasn't what it could be today, I'll tellya that."

Finkelstein said, "That's not good."

"Cool lead in to *Gimme Shelter*, man, you talked all over it."

"Strictly casual format, what can I tell ya?"

"You can respect artists and listeners and hold the jockjive. It's called broadcast etiquette."

"Oh my God, man."

"I'm a firm believer in jockjive not trespassing tunes. Pain of prosecution even."

Finkelstein got a smirk on: "This from the man busted phoning a bombthreat to scuttle a telethon!"

"Hey muva!"

"Community radio saves, man. Feel the magic."

"I dunno, man. While back me 'n' Betty Booty were in a shower in the Ninth Ward, somebody we could hear half a block away~I mean his ass was over his shoulders in a big way~jammin jockjive so bad he couldn't record *Ummagumma*."

"Ass over shoulders in the Ninth Ward? Talk to me, P Doop. What's it take to clean up a thing like this before somebody names it? You tell me what it is I can do."

"You really wanna know?"

"You tell, I shall."

"Let the music play, man. That's all you gotta do. Just let the music play."

"Okay, here's the deal. Earliest opportunity a Stones request timeslot goes out to you and all our good OZ listeners out the Ninth Ward. Plus a copy of *Ummagumma* recorded by me personally for your entertainment or distribution. Now I ask you: How's that for making the pain go away?"

"Whodat everybody's favorite unindicted rock jock?"

Voice called, "Cottonmouth!" Somebody screamed. Finkelstein and Poopdeck Perry scrambled up and away. Tex Rowe and Flat Annie were packing and pulled—Flat Annie a snubnose 38, Tex a Buntline Special—but calmer heads prevailed and pieces pointed away.

Feet of OoooseBadoose was this big snake out of no-where, switchbacked centerfront the crosslegged man. OoooseBadoose perked brow with notice. Barely a twitch man or snake.

Somebody spoke up, "Uh, I don't think it would be too cool to stick around, man."

OoooseBadoose said, "Snakes come to me."

Looks crossed, then voices:

What did he say?

First time ever I understood what he said, I still don't know what he's talking about.

Nothing sudden.

With this cottonmouth at his crotch OoooseBadoose spoke calmly and listeners kept wide berth.

OoooseBadoose said, "This is not life and death, this is life not death."

Tex said, "Maybe you know what you know, if nobody else here knows any better, but the question is: Does the snake know it too?"

OoooseBadoose took reflective: "When I was a boy I was struck by lightning. I had this vision of this snake in the grass. Even this moonlight is like I remember."

Milo spoke out, "Snake across the River Styx."

Flat Annie Pratt said, "Where the hell you spozzat thing came from?"

Tex said, "Most poisonous snake in North America middle a Jackson Square? You can't tell me somebody didn't put that thing here."

Joe Bananas said, "Hey, them weeds riverside the levee they crawlin wit snakes, you kiddin me? Pilings under the wharves. Aw man."

Proffit said, "Snake could crawl across Decatuh Street in a storm drain, wouldn nobody be da wizah."

Shushubaby said, "The man who locks these gates, Willie Pickett, he says he won't come in here anymore cuz he saw a big snake one morning. Now I see where Willie Pickett is at."

Milo said, "Practically a parable in our midst. Snake outta nowhere, people all around, snake finds snakepeople. How soulful is that?"

Hidden Dave said, "It's like the old oriental story some village some snake parts a crowd and stops at the feet of somebody holy."

Sidewinding shift to the crook of the man's crossed ankles put a hush on the snakewatch.

Bated stillness.

OooseBadoose spoke: "This is no ordinary turn of events. Realtime planet bearings make like a snake, here's this snake from a lightningbolt of my youth."

Some hippie chick went, "Trip me out!"

OooseBadoose said, "You figure perennial symbols always apply, from a lightningbolt of yesteryear to that snake in the stars and this one on the ground, that's figurative evolutionary current writ large and then some. I'm seeing a turn for the truth in the offing here. Forget Kingdom Come for the Chosen Few. Truth is always enough to go around. One plus one equals one is the proof. Universe to omniverse begins and ends one. That means everybody."

Same hippie chick same flair: "Far out!"

Voice was heard, "Say fuckin what?"
Other voice: "Weird, man."

The woman with snakes and the man in peestained
floodlength candystripe pants were making the northside
gate off the plaza: an object glimpsed at a hole under some
pavement, on closer look, was snakeslough. Man said, "Of
all things to turn up here of all places. Snakes 'n' more
snakes as it is—now even a leftover snake. You know what
that means, doncha? Snakeskin you're lookin at means a
bigger snake you're lookin out for." Snakeskin handover
him to her happened full arm reach of each, room enough
to call good between him and empty snakeskin, same as
any skin full of snake. Her palmhold of absentee snake
stirred the livebodies across her bosom, ripples one, a twitch
the other.

They paid OooseBadoose a curiosity call. Made him an
offering of the snakeslough they had found when they
found out some snake had found him. As for the snakeslough,
if only by crosslooks of a mind, the snake of origin and the
one at the man's feet got to be one and the same snake,
consensus understood.

Luman Harris said, "Snake leave outtiz skin leavin outtiz
hole ain't goin back way it come from, you can call 'at
law."

Bebe, head help upto Buster Holmes', say, "That snake
on the move."

OooseBadoose said, "Nobody here is closer to home."

Bebe hung it mug *What he said?*

OooseBadoose said, "If you believe like Christ believed
that knowing the truth sets you free, most likely you stand

pro snake on Eden, much like He most likely did. That's all I'm saying."

Somebody said, "Man, you really believe anybody believes all that makebelieve anymore?"

OooseBadoose said, "Believe it or not, I think you're about to find more and more seekers revisiting Eden, and numbers of these seekers discovering that Eden encodes atomic memory. It's like this cosmic shellgame with storyline misdirection on the order of virtual sleight of mind: Truth attack rocks Eden; Lord God wants wise who owns the act; Adam and Eve pass blame and then Lord God pulls rank. And what it comes down to is an archetypal ensemble in a dreamscape metaphor of subatomic shadow. And as dreamscape Eden unfolds, downcycle symbols, and symbols within symbols, distill pure symbol, decoding self realization. So you see, dreamscape Eden is more than a place, dreamscape Eden is a symbol of psyche. And the more dreamscape Eden you see by its nuclear light, the more it occurs to you: Awyeah, I remember now."

Dockery took mock indignant: "Who is this debunker of original sin who would have us renounce our guilt?"

OooseBadoose said, "Realize what I'm saying. Eden is not about temptation and not about sin, it's a truth attack on a power trip, plain and clear. It's Perennial Wisdom in the shape of a snake witnessing unresolved ego of a lesser god and a jealous one. Truth is, if anything, the snake upholds our birthright and soul mission to witness truth. I say it's a bum rap been on the Snake this entire epoch. The misread is so integral to the collective arrest I could see some sort of pro snake renaissance heralding the endtime of the age as we know it."

Milo said, "We the people find the defendant not guilty but innocent by reason of native innocence."

OooseBadoose said, "You figure Divine Memory is the seed of the dreamfield, distillation of the symbols of the dreamfield puts the lie to separation."

Albert Johnson pumped soulfist: "Dream baby dream."

OooseBadoose said, "Outside of that, this crescent of a riverbend (where the river makes the magic) can only assume added dimension in a moon cycle figuratively potent as this. Misdirection to end all misdirection can be divined in this sleight of land falling on this moontide. Imagine by the wake of the moon of the snake one fertile crescent reconciles another."

Milo said, "Moonswoon uplink: holocination in progress."

OooseBadoose said, "Snake medicine (redeemed from antiquity), sleight of land on moontide, that's a spiral."

Milo said, "Coming soon to a river near you."

OooseBadoose said, "Out here on the crescent (where the river makes the magic) misdirection imprints the operative sabbath. When or where but daybreak east over the westbank to hallow the pilgrimage of the twiceborn west to Eden? Imagine by the wake of the moon of the snake one fertile crescent reconciles another."

Snake medicine!

Stone zone name alone.

Let's talk buzz immaculate.

OooseBadoose said, "Hallucination of one seeming many turning holocination of all being one immaculation enough?"

Thus spoke Doctor Doose the Revelator of PreHoly NOLA.

OooseBadoose zoned off: "Snake in Eden, snake in a lightningbolt, snake in the solar system, snake at Jackson Square: same snake each snake, waxing allsnake."

Luman Harris went away shaking his head: "Man mightcould be gone back all the way with his recollection. He *got* back some recollection he do."

The snake had not moved, stone still in crook of crossed ankles. Hard to tell was it moonplay on snakeskin or skinplay by moonlight or crossplay whichway; anyway, first blush made solidbody dark, then dappled, then mixcolor petalpattern; some chestnut overtones, some coppertone highlight . . .

Beverly Griffin said, "Maybe somebody awta put the snake in the river."

Fiddler Ron said, "Hey, you wanna save this snake or sacrifice it?" (He had been shown the door at Ruggerio's for asking a diner down on a fish platter how was the PCP.)

Liz said, "All these people packing heat, I dunno, I just don't see this snake leaving here alive."

United Cab Ronnie said, "I think we can all agree on a cease fire here. Everybody cool with that? Nobody greases the snake?"

Tex had that Buntline Special more pulled than packed, he said, "Snake heads for my mother's son gets here short one head he even takes a notion."

Bev said, "You wanna kill that snake so bad."

Woman with snakes said, "That snake has a mother same as your mother's son."

One of the women said, "Yeah, Tex. You behave yourself, you fucker you."

Tex heard that all eyeball; mock brow hung the woman with snakes   *honey, for a poke of what's under them snakes on you my two shots would sound like one*   samebreath subsense   *for a bunktop pile of that action I'm a snakecharmin fool*   he did down with his piece (kept cocked) and called his action packed.

Was a biker could've sworn that snake down the man's feet made with a ripple.

Herecome Poopdeck Perry say, "The weirdest thing just happened."

Tex Rowe said, "Snake here outta nowhere, folks steppin on eggshells, you wanna tell us something weird just happened?"

Poopdeck Perry said, "I just saw Newberry."

Voice said, "Newberry?"

Poopdeck Perry said, "He was across the street, front of the fountain, truck passed between us, he was gone. Then when I turned he was at the gate. Fuckin Newberry, man, I shitchu not. Near to me as I am to you. There and gone then there he was again."

Tex told Poopdeck, "Well I'll tellya one goddamned thing, if I see Newberry, you won't see me. I got my hands full here in this world. Later for that afterlife stuff."

OoooseBadoose spoke up: "Generally speaking, disincarnate beings do tend to be more visible by moonlight, by the way."

Dockery asked, "Seen any disincarnate beings in this light, have you?"

OoooseBadoose said, "I have noticed the tree that statue supplanted."

Dockery said, "What wuzzat now?"

"The tree that stood where the statue stands. I have seen this tree in the *GreatGoneBefore*. It is given to me to do this."

Hidden Dave Crossway said, "No mystery a snake knew snakepeople on this lot."

Dockery said, "A deduction subject to proof, I trust."

Hidden Dave said, "Fearless quality of the seer seeing the seen. You figure mindblinding fears would be at a minimum with a seer seeing the GreatGoneBefore, that nonfear would be the nonresistance to usher a snake to snakepeople. No fear, no threat."

Somebody said, "Man, you're about enough to make me believe what I'm seeing."

Somebody else said, "Notice that *about* slipped in with that *enough?*"

Tex Rowe just shook his head: "I'll be goddamned if this ain't the goddamnedest thing."

Man in the peestained floodlength candystripe pants heard that: "Be goddamned wouldn't I be goddamned too."

"He was there, man. I'm tellin ya. Fuckin Newberry, man. I swear to God."

Can a UFO be far?

Oh hush.

IV

The Crescent

Snake he tell it true
Lord He know it too
Ain't Adam, ain't Eve
Ain' fess up they troofs
Jess give up they kin
Ain't fess, blame jess

Landsake alive, landsake alive
Landsake alive talk about jive

  —*"Epitaph Blues"*
  by Bootlip Russell

Pale of foredawn, arc of the morning star: west reach of moontide down the town.

(*Riverside snorer riffs off a breeze*)

Foreshadowings of a sceneshift stirred onsquare. Round OooseBadoose retreating onlookers backpedaled on tiptoe not to alarm the snake.

Liz Klutch reflected, "Well for something not necessarily a happening thing this certainly did happen in happening ways."

Beverly Griffin said, "Right as you say that I'm getting off on my back not aching like it was."

Woman with snakes spoke up: "Anybody notice the clock has stopped but the chimes still keep the hour?"

Bev said, "Happening in a happening way I didn't know was happening."

Liz said, "Well feature this, dears. Do you realize those dials read maximum waximum?"

Bev said, "For real?"

Liz said, "Moontime to the minute, dear."

Bev said, "Lights out was one thing, now that is something else."

Liz said, "Is that weird or is that weird?"

Bev said, "That is weird."

OoooseBadoose spoke up, "Stoptime at moontime, chimetimes on realtime, betweentime keeps time out of mind—that's a timepiece."

Bev said, "No doubt music of the spheres have nothing on those chimes."

Woman with snakes said, "That's interesting. You mention deep music. It occurred to me those chimes toll token time. Then I got this full fathom impression of the downmost deep rags musicmakers pick up on from the very life pulse of the very living land."

Liz nodded, "Rag mama rag."

Woman with snakes said, "And not just any pulse or any soil either, I mean heartland pulse of continental shed. Rag out these bottoms rag like noplace anywhere ever. Turns of tune to call hearts home."

Liz said, "Purely American art form, by the way."

Woman with snakes said, "Indeed I do believe ragtime off Basin Street to blues out the delta sound off Beulahland proud as any ring shout."

Bev said, "Totally."

Woman with snakes said, "What occurs to me now is wholesale misuse leaving this soil in such a state the music loses its spook. You would think the powers that be have been time immemorial worrying each other who gets to ruin everything. Nowdays this soil is so undercharged any music out of it could only be uninspired. That keeps up this place music comes from could get to be just another place music comes to."

Liz said, "Bummer."

Bev said, "Actually, what I've heard, between chimes, much as anything, is laughter."

Woman with snakes said, "Hallelujah and bless our souls. Laughter between those chimes is no token, sugar; laughter between those chimes is the truth."

Liz said, "Children, you just testified."

Woman with snakes said, "Earth is my witness, by moonblue on the tree of life, to Eternal Spirit, with all my heart, I pray that the beat goes on."

Liz and Bev said amen to that.

Pauline DeSilva said to Poopdeck Perry, "You know, if you ask me, I could swear there's something strange in the air, I've been feeling it in fits and starts all night long."

Poopdeck Perry said, "When the feeling you start fits something in the air, you can swear all night long you're uptight outtasight."

Pauline said, "Uh hunh. So you saw a ghost they're saying?"

Poopdeck Perry said, "That or a double."

Pauline said, "Probably not many people you can talk to about this sort of thing, I would imagine."

Poopdeck Perry said, "I'd imagine a fair number of ghosts don't wanna hear it either."

Pauline said, "Well, let me tell you, you talk about ghosts, a very dear friend of mine, right over here on Kerlerec Street, I won't mention her name, well she swears on all that's holy she owes her life to the ghost of a young boy who woke her up in a house on fire."

Poopdeck Perry said, "Worlds cross here. What can I say? All kinds of stories like that around here."

Pauline said, "Well, I can't say I can attest to that from experience, perse, but I am at least open to the idea that such things are possible, I mean, really and truly, I'm sure these things do happen, afterall, whether or not to me personally, but, anyway, like I say, when people I respect make these claims like I've mentioned, why I take these people at their word; I mean, afterall, who am I to say?"

Poopdeck Perry said, "Hey, well thanks for not thinkin I'm crazy."

Pauline said, "Well, not for that, anyway. Just kidding."

Big Jim Bullshit got a crusade on. See could he get Marlies shut of Immigration. Come Monday would Marlies be out visa coverage. Been all night lowdown sorry and sad down The Boss Fix and now out here down the grass.

Big Jim was talking naturalization infatuation.

Pauline DeSilva was taken back: "You mean marry an american she may not even know just to stay in this country?"

Big Jim Bullshit said, "That's the attraction."

Junior had to laugh: "Lord Jesus have mercy."

Big Jim Bullshit said, "Amen to that, bro. Show me a gay samaritan willing to say I do, I'll show you a savior bringin mercy to burn, know what I'm sayin?"

Milo did Bogart: "Not checkered record enough most couples I've married ended up divorced, now this."

Big Jim Bullshit said, "Listen off, man, other marriages got other aims, hey, long as intentions are tight, man, same difference, know what I'm sayin? We can help Marlies out, we help Marlies out. Capiche?"

Junior said, "I dunno izzit upto Mama Roux or else The

Fallen Angel it's B Drinkers say: 'No way in Hell but all the way here.' You heard that?"

Big Jim Bullshit said, "No way in hell but all the way here. Yeah you right, bro. B Drinkers upto Fallen Angel wear that out, sameway upto Mama Roux. Hey, you heard what OoooseBadoose said about it's nothin like a sunrise wedding down by the riverside. You heard that, right?"

Milo got a grin: "Truly the babblings of an incorrigible romantic."

Scan Nieman ran found a longwayfromhome look from otherside of truth. Marlies saw Nieman coming.

"Pardon me, but I was gonna say, if you remember me from that other place earlier, I'm Art Nieman, by the way, and I just wanna apologize for that."

Marlies hung mug *Why me, Lord?*

"I know, I don't blame ya. I did get kinda weird on ya there, I guess."

Eye contact call no time for double jeopardy.

"Anyway, I just wanted to reprimand myself for that."

She kept shooting glances direction of Miss Buddy and Big Jim Bullshit. Not that he was about to leave it go anytime soon.

"Actually, the thing with me, if you wanna know, I'm more or less between self concepts, you might say. In other words, what I'm sayin is, that incountry cowboy act you saw catch the bum's rush before, well that got smoked out for false impersonation by of all people a Jungian streetsweep. Come right down to it gettin found out like that actually turned out to be somewhatuva relief, I'd say. I mean it's like the Nam fixation can wear on ya like a long march in no long time, believe me, I know. Code name all pack and no mission that detail. I mean you can go only so long puttin over a lie as good as the truth long as you stick to it, next thing you know the assumed identity is hands down more hassle than whatever it is you're running from to assume it. Group therapy one time I even got this curse put on me. I kid you not. Wellwisher was a Nam vet, needless to say. Went off on me humpin these assumptions I made my own use of war stories he'd given out in session, y'know. Wanted he should jump up bad on me, right? Says to me he says, 'I curse you on yourself.' Heavy as any words I ever heard laid on anybody. I curse you on yourself. I thought that was a pretty up 'n' walkin oath myself. Anyway, awhile ago I guess I musta nodded out over here, I had this dream I'm at like this nude beach in Santa Cruz, right? So this holy fool makin with the snake pit act over here, he's there and he says to me, 'A man cursed on himself wants to reflect on his true divine nature.' Now me I'm somebody I'm hip to dreams, right? He scopes me realtime, he scopes a reflecting fool.

"I've digressed. Better I ramble on foot than ramble at the mouth, I suppose, uh? Adios now."

Marlies said, "Take it easy."

Nieman said, "What was that?"

Marlies said, "Take it easy?"

Nieman said, "You're not pissed off?"

Marlies said, "From jungle patrols to here it is far, yah?"

Nieman hung mug *whoa baby now*

Big Jim Bullshit took his talent search underground:

Put a pitch, Miss Buddy broke it down whatfor: "Believe it or not, babycakes, in my time of dying, I did have my go at the marriage thing, and not just once but twice. Well let me tell you, honey, after that first one, Judgment Day could only be a cakewalk, and, mind you, the second one even made the first look good. That's just my rub with the true sense of the word—nevermind this proposition you're making with here."

Big Jim Bullshit said, "C'mon, man, you know how these things go down. I mean let's face it. Who hasn't heard of foreigners legal by wedlock to gay talent they never see? Common knowledge as common law. It's a getover, man. It's a papercaper. Besides that, I might awta mention, between you 'n' me now, it's not like it's just Marlies cops a plea here, y'know."

Miss Buddy said, "Oh, get serious."

Big Jim Bullshit said, "Hey, I am serious. Listen off, man. Genuine marriage certificate sways sympathy of the court your way, you walk off that vice rap you're lookin at, you know what I'm sayin?"

Miss Buddy said, "That's close. As if my final bachelor dissipation were The House of Abandon Revue. Come on now. The defense resting on that could forget order in the court."

Big Jim Bullshit said, "Okay, here's the thing, okay? This is the thing. I mean it's not like it's some heavy speakin part gets laid on ya here, okay? I mean, all you gotta do is say I do and wheel away in a blaze a good will, simple azzat. No risk, no obligations—you don't even hafta be friends. You go back to your life and leave Marlies hers'n, don't nobody suffers. Worse comes to worst, vows outta somebody hellbent for penitentiary time, it's a righteous ass gets put away in stir."

Miss Buddy said, "You sonuvabitch. And just what do you propose I wear on such short notice?"

The moon vigil dispersed. Exodus offsquare, across Decatur Street, on up the levee for daybreak. (Sceneshift up crescent would buttnaked bodies and beerdrinking bikers be carryover concessions to immodest behavior.)

The woman with snakes had the air of a psychopomp heading a following on up the crescent.

Was Milo said these people must be true believers; Albert Johnson would say *apotheosii*; OooseBadoose, holy host.

Allnight moonlighters waiting for the sun.

Folks left OooseBadoose keep vigil him and the snake root of the raintree. He would swear to something of a subscale marking more or less like a thunderbolt visible now and again on closer looksee. The snake never flinched when he bowed down low, then got to his feet and stood looking down, then turned on his heels and walked away.

Peach offering left lay downspread of snakeskin: icon *self concept out of ego into conscience*

Last he looked the snake was still there.

He slowwalked on up the levee.

Marlies was not ready to do this thing naked, nor was Miss Buddy if he had to be a man. Not that Marlies in waitress wear would be putting any floor service look to the touch. But OooseBadoose insisted no way would it do for a son of Adam to take vows in drag. Then Miss Buddy came by a caftan whose donor (afterclad in all of a jockstrap) scored safe conduct to wardrobe options by means of United Cab Ronnie.

Offside the crescent where the river makes the magic:

Luman Harris brought Hutch onto the levee in observance of a ceremony to go down on the hoof. A slowrolling southbound sealed off The Moonwalk.

People took places down cement steps to the water. The Holy River aummed unstruck sound. Only the slowrolling southbound broke silence. Mud vapors aired trace heartland. Somewhere a rooster crowed.

OooseBadoose sounded over the face of the waters:

I bow to the light within
I bow to the light in all that is
I bow to Eternal Spirit, Ancient of Days
I bow to the Oracle within, to all Guides in Spirit
and to all Allies in the Light;
I bow to all Seeking Spirits on all shining paths
I bow to all lineages of Adepts who have passed
Divine Wisdom thru the Ages
I bow to Elemental Spirits and Devas in the World of Light
I bow to presiding Deities and Consorts,

to presiding Gods and Goddesses,
    and to other High Spirits in all realms of the Universe
I bow to Perfected Beings beyond death

Thank you Grandfather for all that is
Thank you Grandmother for all that you give
Thank you for this lifetime
Thank you for this day
Thank you for now and forever
Salaam
Sat Nam
Amen

As the sun broke east over the westbank Marlies and Miss Buddy descended the steps to strains of Daytime Johnny Omen and Jivin Jeff Dean down on a doowop: ". . . *I met my little browneyed doll / down byyy the ri-ver-side / down byyy the riii-verrrr-siiide* . . ."

Up the Moonwalk Hutch brayed a big *EEEEE-AAAWWWNNNK.*

Tex Rowe called out, "Even the mule can't keep a straight face, BJimBu."

Bottomstep where feet felt water Marlies and Miss Buddy faced Milo in early sun:

"Do you Son of Adam pledge your worth growing your soul and witnessing this Daughter of Eve growing hers?"

"I do."

"And do you Daughter of Eve pledge your worth growing your soul and witnessing this Son of Adam growing his?"

"I do."

"By birthright vested in Children of God I pronounce you one and one are one."

Marlies and Miss Buddy embraced to applause.

(Was then Pauline DeSilva with a glance off cathedralway picked up on the clock back on time.)

Good wishes and cheer went out to Marlies whose longwayfromhome look had given over to rapture of a daughter of Eve in the city of her soul. Yonder sunrise over Algiers, tugboat and barge tandem outlined in offglory out midstream, preholy NOLA broke bath of gold.

OoooseBadoose tranced on the closing prayer: "Now hear this: It is accomplished. One fertile crescent reconciles another. Our ritual harmony we commend to self fulfillment. As for our diaspora ending where it began? When you take the sun for atomic memory excarnate, that's subatomic shadow dispelled in your face. What then becomes of the world appearance? Make no mistake about it: the seer seeing that not that sees for real. At any rate, speaking of appearances, by this sun over this fertile crescent, fellow pilgrims west to Eden, twice blessed all of us, we praise Eternal Spirit, all respects due."

Amen understood

Amen the amen of hardly anybody listening anyway but young hearts in good faith afterall

That sort of amen

When OoooseBadoose left off the crescent, back over the square, the snake was gone. Peach seed was all was left of the offering on snakeskin to root of the golden raintree (sweet part gone the way of somebody going with God). He stood looking down where the snake had been; inspiration   *hallow snake renaissance hallow*

Meantime, the weddingparty powertaxied by Harley hogs down Got Grease down Decatur Street.

Timetrappin Tom, man, he could fix a broken
egg and send it out, no way would anybody know.

—Tommy Blaha

Hash house Got Grease down old Decatur Street opposite
The Boss Fix Jam. Featuring Master Grill and Deepfry
Chef Timetrappin Tom Hill with protege Tommy Blaha
(whose pearldiving gig to work off pinball repairs had
upgraded to weekend short order specialist).

Couple redeye regulars: Doc greasing down after a produce
offloading gig round the French Market; and Willie Woe in
tanktop and boxershorts, all told a Willie Woe story over his
head: "I wake at sun up, I couldn't believe it, the window
was open and my pants were gone. I'm been broke into and
my pants been took. You believe 'at shit? My pants for
chrissake! Didn't mess with my tutu; didn't take my shoes.
Didn't even lift my billfold or my bottom dollar out of it. All
they took was my pants! I mean how offthewall can you get?
Here I'm depantsed till the thrift shop opens. I mean hey,
y'know, come on, I mean gimme a break."

Blaha said, "Whozzat gonna mess with no tutu you ain't
got, Willie Woe?"

Willie Woe said, "Hey, wadn' long figgin 'at out, wuz
ya? I can see howcome you got way you at."

Tommy said, "Any tutu you got wouldn't nobody want
anyway."

Willie Woe said, "What's got into you, boy? Puttin the
shit to a man what's been depantsed. Whattayou, crazy?"

Commotion of Harley hog action out the bus stop. Doc
ran a counterstool scan on the swivel. Specter of outlaw
bikers not to be stared down, clearing Miss Buddy and Big

Jim Bullshit; also the familiar Mespero's waitress a rumbleseat legshot to the Mojave Desert referral of moon yore.

Timetrappin Tom said, "Uh oh. Here comes Big Jim Bullshit."

Willie Woe said, "If I'm underdressed already, I feel naked now."

Miss Buddy leaned in: "Counter reservation for the Bullshit weddingparty?"

Timetrappin Tom said, "You're a moonbleached bunch ever I saw some!" Bringing on freshbrewed joe as he spoke.

Doc said: "Mojave Desert!"

Biker said: "Sweep 'n' scoop!"

"You got it."

The reception spanned counterfront. Good coffee kept coming. Ones who were there broke it down for the ones who were not.

Miss Buddy said, "Put it this way. Even a snake got to be there."

Marlies said, "And go away."

Miss Buddy said, "This is true."

And Marlies said, "Free to come and free to go."

Timetrappin Tom nodded, "Even a snake."

Miss Buddy said, "Even a snake."

Willie Woe said, "Am I the only one who *did* sleep but *didn't* dream all night?"

Miss Buddy said, "Talk to us when you figure out are you in or out of bed, babycakes."

Willie Woe said, "Somebody ripped off my pants, okay? How you think I feel about it?"

The Beadlady leaned in, Blaha froze her: "Don't ask!" and she didn't. She went away.

Big Jim Bullshit said, "Buddy a mine been a long time knowin her swears he seen her put off a mexican bus."

Timetrappin Tom said, "Concentrum complex goin on there, bless'er soul."

Big Jim Bullshit said, "Been hip to the cajun a-rab riff she's puttin on the street lately?"

Timetrappin Tom said, "Beadspeak with a splash of coonass! Now that mightcouldbe somebody I could call a musicmaker."

They got down on hashbrowns and grits like only Timetrappin Tom could sling.

Blaha decanted Abita Springs Adam's ale.

Timetrappin Tom lifted a toast: "To Citizen Marlies."

"*Fuckin A!*"

Certain folks all night with this moon faced daybreak covered in moonprints. Some kept vigils according to their views.

Moonwalk benchtop: the two live ones passed out in each other's arms; Dockery here to see to it they didn't get rolled; tableau diehard native son, bending even unlistening ears: "Yeah, now Napoleon House, see, now that place has this kind of a warp figment air about it, y'know. Like any given moment you could see shades of Sherlock Holmes playing chess with Kafka. Night time bartender there, fella name of Bob Parker, practically defies comparison. Hands down the best act I've seen behind a bar. I mean you haven't laughed till you've seen what his nazi soul routine does to a Wagner crescendo. I've seen him squeeze off a tear at full length nazi salute. No way you could care less whatcher laugh says aboutcha, that's how funny this guy is. Hardly a naziphile's naziphile either, I might add—y'know that perverse sort of fascination some people have? Well Parker regards the Fuhrer a wayward romantic. His thing is they shoulda let Hitler into art school. Nevermind it begs thwarted artistic ambitions mutating to Third Reich and Second World War proportions. This is no ordinary proposition; in fact, if you ask me, it's something more on the order of an enchantment."

Luman Harris and Old Hutch they left off the crescent, slowslow walking, attitude *done been* On out Elysian Fields clear to Desire; hearts in song to the pattern of the hoofbeats: "*Children of Our Lord Finding Our Way to the Ford.*" Hymns would come as man and mule went. On up Freret Street

some boys fell in step, they sang right along. Well Luman
and Old Hutch they just loved that. Children of Our Lord
finding their way to the ford.

PeeCandy in floodlength knew what he knew. No hangover.
No shakes. Must of went out of him while the river turned
when moon did.

"That woman with the snakes, you seen'er have ya?"

"I could swear she was right over here just a moment
ago."

"Been lookin all over for her."

"Gee, I dunno, man."

How to figure a woman easy as her to look at could pass
notice and just fade from view simple as that? No sooner
there and had been than not there and not about to be. Man
wound up stretched out same bench stirred from turn of
moontide.

Milo took Nieman by Maison Bananas where his truck was
parked right remove from *No Parking At No Time* painted
on the sidewalk. They tooled up St. Charles Avenue to
Carrolton and bellied counterside Camillia Grill for
omelettes.

Then they cut over Milo's place out La Bature.

Squatter shanty, shade of willows, riverside the levee.
Bottomland zone patch culled from a nicklebag found out
St. Louis Street by Leo Dazzolini who had no truck with
the stuff but figured Milo might.

They took backporch hammocks looking out wide
water.

Nieman woke on floorboards under the hammock. No Milo other hammock, smell of coffee inside. Nieman told Milo this dream he had he was a new wave native working on the street crew.

Milo said, "Cool dream guardians!"

Time came Hidden Dave and Shushubaby cut over La Marquis for an alsatian pigout (coffee and croissants). After that they cut over her place and wound up down on the thinking stiff's cure.

To somebody like him strung out on hippie arrogance somebody like her would come off refreshing:

"A house with a yard. Some flowers. Some friends."

"You're a poet."

"There you go bullshitting again."

"There you go blushing. Again."

"You're embarrassing me."

"I see that."

"Well stop."

"No."

In The GreatAllBecoming One For The GreatGoneBefore

Evening stroll with Shushubaby and his mom, they're on his either arm: mom trips up, drops flat on the pavement; and then however defiant of odds, somehow Shushubaby crosswipes on top of her—sudden as that he's at this standstill over these women in a heap at his feet . . . How this downturn from promenade to pileup was even mathematically possible he would never know

The man and the moment met on St. Peter Street.

Before OoooseBadoose could say Ooosebadoose, some beautiful person slipped him a fin.

Thought caught   *evolved panhandling threshold the snake renaissance*

No shoes/no service left him outside A&P looking in. Was Fiddler Ron brought coverage: "I'll fly if you buy." He was on.

Shadeside the golden raintree down Jackson Square they got down on milk and chocolate chip cookies and called it food of the gods. Was Fiddler Ron brought up about the snakeskin been lifted; eyecontact calls crossed brokenfield: wise of eyes, OoooseBadoose knew was Fiddler Ron ate the peach; eyes otherwise, Fiddler Ron knew OoooseBadoose knew what he knew.

(Crosscalls within crosscalls)   *thieves who munch offerings on behalf of Eternal Spirit are not exactly thieves (if not saints either)*

Liz Klutch and Mary Mosley joined Pauline DeSilva for coffee. Balconyside they signified on Sunday morning coming down. Pauline rhapsodized of hearing their pushcart and brooms in the night and sometimes watching Liz and the boys sweep the plaza. It intrigued Pauline that their moonswoon vigil may have originated with something Albert said.

Pauline said, "Well what about the one with the muscles who talks to people? I don't believe I saw him here."

Liz and Mary crossed looks. Liz said, "Too wired, dear," and Mary agreed.

Liz got down on war stories from the *GreatGoneBefore*:

"*First* thing in the morning I get shaken awake in bed. *Tommy* has a game with this softball team that he plays on. Would I take him?"

Mary Mosley shook her head: "I couldn't share a balcony with him."

"Tell me about it, dear. I couldn't believe it. Ten o'clock in the morning I'm driving to Metairie. Of course Tommy knows the way, right? *Three times* we had to stop and ask directions. *Fi*nally Tommy sees this game going on at this field we're passing on the way someplace else. Well I mean to tell you this place was a *prairie*. No cover, no trees, no shade of any kind. We're up in like these bleacher seats, okay? *Hot!* I mean it was in*tense*! Well you can imagine what it's like trying to watch a game with him. The whole time he's like yelling at their manager or whatever: 'Put me in, dammit, put me in.' I'm like, Tommy, for heavensakes, has it occurred to you that getting here on time might've improved your chances of getting in the game? Well, do you know, after all that hassle, he didn't get to play. Not one single inning. Well. First three rows move back. I mean *he* ranted. *He* raved. *He* threw his mitt in the bayou. I said, Great, Tommy, that's just great. Take it out on the mitt. *He* had to climb over a *seven foot Page fence* to go get that mitt out of the bayou. It was unreal. He . . . was like . . . a little . . . kid. It was unreal."

Pauline said, "A rather intense young man, I would say."

Liz said, "Oh, you can say that again, dear."

Mary said, "He's a trip."

They were enjoying one another.

Mary said, "Don't look now, but there's Dickinthedirt."

Pauline said, "There's who?"

Mary said, "Sorry."

Liz said, "A friend of ours."

Mary amended that: "Somebody we know, put it that way."

Liz said, "Only too well, I'm afraid."

Mary said, "Oh shit."

Liz said, "He sees us."

Mary said, "Why me, Lord?"

Dickinthedirt called from the plaza below: "Hey Liz."

Liz said, "Hello, dear."

Dickinthedirt said, "Hey, you seen Newberry?"

Liz said, "Newberry's dead for heavensake. You know that."

Dickinthedirt said, "Not Newberry. Izzat who I said?"

Mary said, "That's who you said, you moron."

Dickinthedirt said, "Hey Mary."

Mary said, "Don't 'hey Mary' me. You knew I was here."

Dickinthedirt said, "I apologize for my imperfections."

Mary said, "Long as you just declare and don't itemize."

Dickinthedirt said, "Not to itemize, but I meant Poop-deck Perry, not Newberry. Seen him any chance? P Doop, I mean."

Mary said to Liz, "Practically a cosmic slip. In the wake of seeing Newberry, P Doop gets misnamed for him. How weird is that?"

Dickinthedirt called up again, "It was P Doop I meant."

Liz said, "Is this weird and getting weirder in a hurry or what?"

Mary said, "You can say that again."

Pauline said, "You might say he gave up the ghost and how. Just Kidding."

Weird getting weirder sudden weirder still, self invite won over dismay—crosslooks waxed tidal as Dickinthedirt buzzed in.

Time came Pauline asked Dickinthedirt, "Pardon me for asking, if I'm not being too personal, but I have to wonder however on earth you came by such an unflattering nickname."

Dickinthedirt shrugged, "Figure of speech just sorta bounced back and stuck, I guess."

Pauline said, "Oh dear. Well personally, if you don't mind my saying so, I find Vernon quite suits you. Otherwise, the endearment, if you will, I find utterly lacking."

Dickinthedirt said, "Might think different knowing I just now woke up under a table at The Funk Shop."

Pauline said, "Well of all the rarefied situations."

Dickinthedirt said, "Truth is I still don't remember how I got there, and how I got out I still don't believe."

Pauline said, "Well if that isn't a caution," and Liz and Mary crossed looks.

Dickinthedirt said, "It's like you wake up, right, no idea where. It occurs to you you're under this table, okay, but what table where remains unclear. I lose interest, right? I'm like, later for this, I shine it on. Maybe I'll care when I wake up again, right? I wake up again, it's like the room it's like moving, right? Then it's the table is what it is like it's moving. Then the floor moving under me, then me moving not the floor. So here I am drug ass from under this table, right? I notice it's The Beadlady has me by the heels. Well you talk about a rude awakening, I'm here to tellya, woke up drug ass by the heels by The Beadlady, that's stone novelty, you can quote me on that. I'm like, You mind telling me what's comin off here? She makes with this weird kinda voice in this weird kinda accent, she goes like: *You wanna buy you a Luckybead else you wanna leave outta town.* I said, You said what? She said, You heard what I said. I said, What you mean umma leave outta town? She said, I meant leave outta town like I said. I said, How come izzat umma leave outta town? She said, On accounna you no fun is howcome izzat. I said, Can't nobody be no fun none azzat. She said, How many funfolk you seen drug ass out under no table lately? I said, Better gimme two Luckybeads. And make that mojo. No future I can see in mere souvenirs. She said, Howbout umma give ya three fa fidollas? Well I had that money across her palm before she was all the way out with the words."

Liz said, "Heavyhanded salespitch she laid on you there."

Mary said, "So where's the fun?"

Dickinthedirt made out pocket with the charms.

Pauline said, "What are those things anyway?"

Dickinthedirt shrugged, "Mardi Gras beads. Cheap plastic."

Pauline said, "Well of all things. Well, you know something, Vernon? Here's what I think. I don't think anybody with a heart like yours should be called you know what you know where, I don't care what for. That's my opinion."

Dickinthedirt said, "Weird, man. I mean here you are Vernon this and Vernon that, I'm like, Vernon? What Vernon?"

Pauline said, "I wonder. Absent my Aunt Kaka, who usually goes with me to mass, bless her soul, do you suppose I could persuade any of you moonlighters to come along?"

Liz and Mary would shake that one off, shine it on.

Dickinthedirt said, "St. Louis Cathedral comin freshdrug offa The Funk Shop floor, what, you tryin to blow my mind or what?"

Pauline said, "I don't know about that, but given a chance, who knows what you may find uplifting?"

Dickinthedirt said, "Do they have a hot choir?"

Pauline said, "Pardon me?"

Mary told Pauline, "Don't waste your time."

Pauline said, "Practically as many souls in the choir as the congregation, if that's any indication."

Dickinthedirt said, "Y'know, on second thought, with a personal mission I could accomplish, I could see busting mass and calling that good."

Pauline said, "*Bust*ing . . . ?"

Liz said to Pauline, "It's called recipe for disaster, dear."

Mary said, "She's right, you know. You really don't wanna

let him ruin your day and maybe somebody else's if you can help it."

Pauline said, "Oh dear."

Liz said, "Don't do it."

Dickinthedirt said, "Talk about flags all over the field."

Mary said, "Oh, hang it up, man."

Dickinthedirt said, "Hey, spiritual eunuchs have feelings too, y'know."

Short busting mass, Dickinthedirt knelt next Pauline, spark a couple candles, one for her Aunt Kaka, other for his friend Newberry.

Father McCready paused to make nice and ask after Aunt Kaka. Bells tolled the hour, Father said, "Time to officiate. Blessings to Aunt Kaka. And blessings on the soul of your friend, Mr. . . ."

Dickinthedirt said, "Quazimodo."

Father said, "Mr. Quazimodo. Now there is a name to hear bells by."

Dickinthedirt said, "Purest thing in the Quarter those bells."

Father nodded: "Cultivated sentiment your Tennessee Williams. Blessings due an exponent of our literary firmament, I'm sure."

Was downdraft to be shook by the look of Dickinthedirt watching the father walk.

Pauline said, "Vernon, you must know I do see the better angels of your nature, but it does get hard to know what to say to you."

"Yeah, well Holy Papa there didn't show me any loss for

words wanting he should insinuate on me like I'm the Hunchback of St. Louis Cathedral or somesuch."

"Frankly, I was a little disappointed in both of you, if you wanna know the truth. Spoofing like that before Sunday morning mass. The unmitigated gall of some people."

Dickinthedirt said, "You gotta get it. This is no hangover headache I got, this is a personality headache."

They agreed they might meet at a discussion group sometime.

Foredawn raid up Lafitte Street Incinerator accomplished relic pushcart turnover Joe Bananas style. Watchman out the yard was a crapshooting crony. Sixpack Joe ponied up was plenty good to keep him looking otherway. All told, Joe drove in with three scrap pushcarts and out with four new and unused.

Meantime Proffit made a comeback up Nellie's up Rampart Street:

Nellie said, "Well, here it is, Bobo. Your time has come."

Proffit said, "Aw yeah? Tell me somp'n good, whydoncha? Spozza be umma git foist refusal of any foreman job come open in Sanitation count ah got highest rating on some Civil Soivice exam. Yeah, top rate foist refusal ma ass. Foreman openin upta Lafitte Street: you think ah got foist refusal? Same widdat openin out Constitution Street. What got refused foist wuz ma foist refusal, at's what got refused, umma teyyadat right nah. Refused even befaw ah could refuse it. Here Little Joe he been head of Operations he ain't never even took no exam. Joe ain't never took no Civil Soivice exam. Joe ain't never took nuttin. I ain't sayin he ain't done a good job. All ahm sayin it's accounna they couldn't bust Little Joe any lower than way ah wuzzat is howcome the openin come ma way at all. Even now ah don't git no foist refusal case ah might refuse. Believe 'at? Otha times ah didn't get no foist refusal case ah might accept, this time ain't no foist refusal case ah might refuse. Nah you tell me how you gonna figya da shit deeze people wanna come out wit, uh?"

Nellie said, "You know somp'n, Bobo. Just between you

'n' me, them hippiz gonna eat Little Joe alive, you know that? They gonna chew him up 'n' spit him out, you wait 'n' see. Little Joe puffin hisself out like he do only gonna give 'em more to chew on. You jess wait 'n' see don't they eat him alive, ahm tellinya."

Proffit said, "Not when them hippiz got you figgid like you got Joe figgid, dey gonna figga you got Joe covered, see? Won't nunnadem dey gonna mess widdat."

Nellie said, "Go home, Bobo Proffit."

Proffit said, "Ah been thrown outta better places."

Nellie said, "First thing you said all night I believe."

Proffit in his truck and Joe Bananas in his put hardproof traffic on the air, signing off none too soon:

"All these years them nitwits up the hall wouldna shit where I've stood, now they wanna gladhand me like some long lost brother caught a break they seen comin all along? Talk about bulltweed on a halfshell—dat's bulltweed on a halfshell at a discount, y'ask me."

"Copydat, Bobo. They could shit in they hats 'n' partyhat to beat the band, ah could care less, me."

Voice busted in Be in his office first thing:

Assistant Director George Rogers, driving his family to church in a Sanitation radio car, copied that traffic. *GreatGoneBefore* not the first time Proffit, or Joe, had blown a break; *GreatAllBecoming* not the last.

When Old Shep got off the slaveship (a bus named Desire) Jake was there at the bus stop waiting.

"*Oooh*, Jake. Whatchu doin you waitin me here, Jake? You waitin me?"

"Ain't nobody waitin nobody, Shep. Ahm here 'n' you comin."

Jake walked Shep down St. Louis Street for Napoleon House.

"Bout fret me did somebody send you to see about me way wuz ahm at, no kiddin."

"Don't nobody send me to see about nobody, Shep. Ahm figgin I'll head on up the levee widdat cigar what ahm brung like y'said wuz y'gonna."

"Whodat said dat bout dat, Jake?"

"So you ain't brung no cigar."

"Ah dunno nuttin bout no cigar ain't ahm brung, Jake."

"Well if this ain't some shit."

"*Oooh!*"

"Yeah, das right. Dis what shitscrubbed looks like richyeh."

"You know ah don't smoke no cigars, Jake. You mixin me wit Greco, you think? You know about Greco smokes them cigars."

"Damnside ain't ahm farnuff upwind what about no cigar ahm spozza git ain't ahm got."

"Ah can tell what's a mixup, Jake. It's a mixup like is hyeh. Whawuzzat you said wuz I said wuz Greco wuzza one said, folla wuttum sayin?"

"Dammit to hell, Shep, you wanna know what's a mixup, I'll tellya what's a mixup. You talkin what's a mixup, *that's* what's a mixup, Shep. Damnside talkin to you don't get to be no dizzy spell, sure as hell I dunno what does, I swear. It's a man could lose his way wuz he goin tryna make some sense outta you, so hep me Gawd."

"Y'know what, Jake? It's somp'n what else. Listen ahm sayin. Don't a night go by don't Greco light up a big fat cigar it's all he can do to smoke down. You seen them kind like he smokes. Oooh, Greco he goes for them great big fat cigars, man. Well y'know it's a fella could pick up alotta cigar what Greco puts out can't he smoke down."

"So who needs a guardian angel it's Greco on his way? Well howbout let's just neveryoumind what about no damn cigar you ain't brung 'n' Greco ain't gonna. Howbout, steadadat, you tell me som'n, Shep. I just wanna know one goddamn thing. All I wanna know is whazzis I heard wuzzit you invented the muffuletta?"

"Whawuzzat I *wha*wuzzit you hoyd?"

"Listen up close, Shep. Umma talk it tuyya slow. Wuz it you invented the muffuletta, like Rangoon Johnny sez it wuz, or wuz it Rangoon Johnny talkin out his ass wuz it you? You tell me, Shep."

"*Urnggh*, Jake, ieyieyie, that Rangoon Johnny, boy, between you 'n' me now, that Rangoon Johnny, he's somp'n else, man. Rangoon Johnny he ain't right, poor fella. Ain't Rangoon Johnny ain't right a little bit Rangoon Johnny ain't. You know it's folks say Rangoon Johnny still talks on his sea legs, man, it's folks say like at, no kiddin. Y'know howzat Rangoon Johnny talks like he talks? Well it's folks say cuzza Rangoon Johnny still talks at talk like he talks izzat howcome it's folks say he's alotta stuff, y'know? It's folks say like at, Jake, you know like ahm sayin? Dis between you 'n' me now, don't say nothin, hear? Ooooh, that wouldn't be good."

"All I know is Rangoon Johnny he says you can ask anybody cept you wuzzit you invented the muffaletta—he says cuzza you fuggot wuzzit you invented it."

"Izzat right? Rangoon Johnny said like at? Poor fella, he's talkin at talk it's folks say like he talks on his sea legs like at, poor fella. You heard like I said it's folks say like at?"

"All I know is Rangoon Johnny he says it just goes to show you just never know. Well I told Rangoon Johnny, I said to'm I said, Here Uncle Stadutti takes all the credit for the muffuletta when all this time wuzzit Shep wuzza one invented it? Well I'll be goddamned don't that sound to me like no muffuletta story ever I heard one."

"You wanna know what's a muffuletta story, I'll tellya what's a muffuletta story."

"By Gawd you know what's a muffuletta story, Shep, well you just go right on ahead, you tell me. Ahm listenin atcha, Shep."

"Yeah, well see, my momma, see, she useta put olive salad on a muffuletta, y'see. You know olive salad? Ooooh, momma she make olive salad some konna good, boy. Ah mean to tell you it was some konna good, *umm hmn.* See, momma she don't hold no sugar out her olive salad, see. Oooh, momma, she lay it on, boy, momma she lay that sugar on, ahm tellin ya. Well it wuzzat good olive salad momma she useta put on a muffuletta, see. Well before Mr. Pete died—you know Mr. Pete, Sal's dad Mr. Pete? Well before Mr. Pete died I give him a bite off a muffuletta like my momma useta make. Well Mr. Pete he wanna know howcome wuzzat muffuletta so good. I tole'im I said wuzzat how ma momma useta make a muffuletta. Mr. Pete he said, Man, would I love to make a muffuletta good eatin azzat. Well, Mr. Pete he wuz my buddy, see. Me 'n' Mr. Pete we wuz like at, see. We buddies me 'n' Mr. Pete we was. So y'see howcome izzat Napoleon House got that good muffuletta like ma momma useta make wuz it all cuzzadat, see . . . (*Urngggh* . . . Listen, uh, Jake. *Uh humn* Teyya what. Howbout don't let's say nuttin bout no sugar, hyeh? You know that sugar in that salad like I said about? Oooh, between you 'n' me now, betta best we leave out about dat. Bout dat sugar ah mean about. Between you 'n' me now)—"

Jake had stopped coming along: steps back, toed curbside, got a prospect on.

"Oooh, Jake. Donchu go smokin no butts out no gutter, you hyeh?"

"The hell?" Read snakeslough in hand.

"Wuzzat you got there, Jake? What izzat?"

"What a man ain't found on these streets wouldn't tally to tell."

"Oooh, Jake. No tellin what izzat. You know what izzat? Hyeeee, Jake, I dunno."

"Damnside no tellin what the hell this is about."

"Hyeeee, Jake, you dunno wuzza alligata man had dat. You know a alligata man?"

"The hell you talkin no alligata man? You dunno nuttin bout no hoodoo, Shep. Don't gimme nunnadis allagata man. Who you tryna kid?"

• • •

Ooosebadoose!

Down sidestreetside Napoleon House, barefoot man in black passing otherway, Shep about flinched when OoooBadoose made Doosespeak. Specter of this appearance handy to mention of some alligator man: mug with Shep was mug not lost on Jake.

Shep said, "Whazzat he says?"

Jake said, "He says he'll live until he dies and never know the reason why."

Jake noticed OoooBadoose noticing the snakeskin.

Was a twohand hold on the snakeskin OoooBadoose brought over the plaza. Gates locked on the square (snake in? people out), pale of the plaza got that display shine on. Threshold OoooBadoose sat facing the cathedral same threshold Albert Johnson once rhapsodized bath of moonlight.

He dozed and when he woke The Beadlady was there. Then Ruthie the Ducklady came passing by.

(A native son lining up local play for live ones could get religion off a moment like this: The Beadlady, Ruthie the Ducklady and OoooBadoose same frame.)

The Ducklady handed over a luckybead and told The Beadlady: "Somebody loss somp'n."

The Beadlady held this luckybead upto looksee. She said, "Everyone is saved by their faith." She kissed the luckybead and passed it back.

The Ducklady went, "Yeah?"

The Beadlady hung mug *got a soul who gets it*

The Ducklady told The Beadlady, "I've always wanted to meet you," she brought her a hug.

Glance The Beadlady cut OoooseBadoose left off unmet; OoooseBadoose dozed down done.

Duck and Ducklady presented proud: "Me I'm Ruthie and this is Flo."

The Beadlady said, "I know who you are," and slumped played out.

Was then OoooseBadoose, bolt wakeful, told The Ducklady, "That's a two dollar luckybead, and nodded off again.

The Ducklady and Beadlady took slack with that. The Beadlady hung her head same as OoooseBadoose.

The Ducklady waved, said, "Bye now," and wandered off, Flo in tow; cornerturn and gone.

Across Decatur Street, by Cafe Du Monde, Ruthie The Ducklady loomed fountainside; peeking not squinting, got a wish on: "I wanna see The Beadlady saved by her faith," she palmed off her luckybead, chased it with a kiss . . .

The Beadlady was gone when OoooseBadoose woke in the night.

Electric shadow ultra solitary: him on the plaza and nobody else.

Foredawn foghorn upriverway, he left off the plaza for daybreak at the crescent: Trance off doom of shadow by sleight of land down holyriverside:

Atomic memory traces this sitting or so much the sooner than later . . .

(Snakeskin down steptop and not in his pants, unaware he had sat on his charm.)

• • •

Titty Window in the GreatAllBecoming

. . . Bywater in the Ninth Ward: Leo Dazzolini offseat a grocery bike: passes some kid tribute to relay across the street . . . Upstairs window big sister profiles whatfor . . . (Next time across the kid's palm plus extra coaxes big sister to shake what she shows.)

I was having a cigarette when the lights went out,
and the weird thing about it, I haven't had one since.

—Amy Conn
aka Shushubaby

A Thinking Stiff's Cure In The GreatAllBecoming:
"You're the first white dude I've been attracted to in a long
time."

"Kennedy speech was what it was."

"That was different all right."

"Got carried away with the inaugural there."

"You said it."

"JFK himself probably never resorted to that for pillowtalk."

"Probably not."

"You tired?"

"Not really."

"Neither am I."

"I never know what to expect from you."

"Neither do I."

"Long as you don't start what you can't finish."

"Sixty minute man goes the distance."

"Full of surprises."

"Satisfaction satisfactual."

"That another Kennedy line?"

"Actually it's Jiminy Cricket."

"Cute."

"Poet's president, JFK, by the way."

Well y'know it got so I just give up tellin about it. Nobody believed it. Hell, half the time I could hardly tell was the recollection plumb or assbent my own damn self. Tell ya one goddamn thing, though, and you can believe this or not. Ever was a night I coulda give up drinkin, hell, even woke up to the truth of the Lord for that matter, by Jesus that was the night. Oh, it's a fetch all right, that'n'then some, by golly, but then again somehow y'know whatcha know, y'know, and that's what I know about that. Anyhow, what coulda been still ain't, I reckon. Me I just give up talkin about it I did. Dammit to hell that's all there is to it . . .

—PeeCandy in floodlength

Where the GreatAllBecoming cross the GreatGoneBefore

Turnout halfdozen strong first thing Monday for a papercaper to beat city hall: Milo flashing credentials and a marriage certificate altogether legal and proper; Miss Buddy appearing in Justice down the hall, more or less handy to lie or to swear to it; Bobo Proffit and Joe Bananas (Sanitation careers flashing before them) about due reckoning with Sanitation brass, Proffit withholding his witness signature but Little Joe fast and loose with his; and hustle architect Big Jim Bullshit down with Marlies down by law . . .

Marlies last seen rumbleseat a lowrider hauling up Tulane Avenue on out Highway 61 . . .

THAT NOT THAT